THE DOOR

By: Ron Mueller

Books by Ron Mueller

The Door

The Savitar Series-Science Fiction
Journey's End
Savitar
Confluence

Bram Nielson Series-Science Fiction
The Fold
The Message
Fold Wormhole
Negative Fold
Ripples in Time

The Alex Evercrest Series-Detective
The River Front
The Girl on the Grill
Missing
Maggot
Racist
Votive Candles
Windy City
Country Road
Pool of Blood
Sins of the Daughter

The Taelo Series-Prehistory America
Taelo: The Early Years
Taelo: The Golden Feather
Taelo: Journey of Discovery
Taelo: Dangerous Passage
Taelo: Condor Clan Slingers
Taelo: Circumvention
Taelo: The Journey of Sages

A Taelo Story
The Name of the Child
White Swan and Quiet Pheasant
Broken Spear
Floating Cloud
Quiet Rabbit
Busy Bee
Little Otter& Talking Wren
Burley Bear & Meadow Flower

A Feather-in-the-Wind Story
The Eastern Elk Clan

The Problem Solver Series-Secret Agent
The Beginning
Drug Lords
Broder Crosser

Current Past and Future-Science Fiction
Event Survivors-Science Fiction
The Door-Science Fiction
Viajante 7-Science Fiction
Imagination by Courtney Huynh and Chloe Parker

THE DOOR

By: Ron Mueller

Around the World Publishing LLC
4914 Cooper Road Suite 144
Cincinnati, Ohio 45242-9998

The Door by Ron Mueller Copyright © 2021
Renewed © 2023

ISBN 13: 978-1-68223-323-8
ISBN 10: 1-68223-323-5

Distributed by Ingram
Cover Picture By: Rolffimages, Dreamstime.com
Cover Design by Ron Mueller

Thank you to my wife,

Hien.

I work for food, and she keeps me well fed.

Table of Content

Introduction

The unimaginable distances of space and the limits of the human life span have always been a major barrier to the exploration of the Solar system and to the wider Universe. Humans have entered into a period where they can see but they have little hope of ever touching.

We continue to probe, to learn and to develop understanding. Finally in much the same way rubber was discovered by accident when a failed experiment was thrown out into the snow or Ivory Soap became the soap that floated by an accident of over stirring, the whim of a brilliant scientist provides the breakthrough in the ability to transport living matter from one location to another.

However, the receiver must be at the desired destination location. Those desired locations are millions and billions of light years apart.

The solar system will be conquered by the DOOR. The universe beyond will still be well beyond the reaches of the human race for eons or until the next experiment of learning to fold time and space can be achieved.

The Doors to space need to be put into position.

This is the story of how it all got started.

Chapter 1: The Door Team

Two goals had come alive when she began to take the challenge of her life seriously. The first was to make a social difference in the standing of women. The second was to pursue her passion for space. She had more or less stumbled into her current level of social involvement. She had not originally planned for or even dreamt of attaining the role she had just been elected to.

She had originally only been interested in getting the inner city kids a chance to grow into productive, happy, working adults and in that process give young women a positive view of themselves.

Her work in Chicago's inner city put her face to face with the white political bosses. She learned to manipulate them and win many of them to her cause. Not because they were altruistic but because she had demonstrated that she could get the young voters to the ballot box.

Then one of those political bosses urged her to run for a state senate seat. He assured her she would win.

She had no clue how he knew this or could promise it, but it fit her desire to have a bigger impact than she was having with her focus of saving one kid at a time. She wanted the system to change for the better and saw it as an opportunity to do so. It surprised her when she won as promised.

She served only one term and then on the death of the senior senator from Illinois to the US senate, she was drafted to run. She had never imagined that she could win. She did but barely cleared the hurdle. She did so by only a few hundred votes and suffered through a recount challenge that confirmed her win.

She was a solid performer and won the next two senatorial elections. She became nationally recognized for her work on changing the policing practices and for pushing a national unified police practices bill. It was known as the MacAdam Bill and was passed and signed into law by the President. It was the first time all police organizations had a common set of practices on how to deal with the public across the entire country.

Then her old curmudgeon supporter urged her to run for the Presidency. Once again, he told her she would win. She figured he had something to do with her winning a seat in the state senate but how could he possibly believe she had a chance to become a candidate for the Presidency!

But here she was, looking out from the oval office at the White House lawn. She thought it was a brutal primary race until she ran against a Republican candidate that hated her for being a woman as well as a Democrat.

The Presidential Race was of a street fighting quality. Policy and what each candidate could do for the country was of little consequence or of any seeming interest to the public. It seemed the public was enjoying the brawl between gender more than worrying about the good of the country.

It was all about personality and sticking it to the insiders in Washington. The ugliness just below the veneer of civility, still resided between the races, the gender bigotry and the rancor religious differences raised, all surfaced as the campaigns stirred the public while trying to create a winning coalition of voters.

Her support from the Black, Hispanic, Muslim communities and her solid support from women repulsed by her adversaries view of women, was just enough to get her elected.

So here she was, her third week in office, looking out at the perfectly manicured White House lawn cut to just the right height and mowed to show a crisscross pattern. The lawn keeper of her personal home would envy the care and attention given this lawn.

The lawn held her attention only because the interview for the leader for her pet project was not going well. She needed a person who in her gut she knew would successfully deliver her pet project. She had interviewed two very qualified candidates that seemed to look great on paper but on a one-to-one basis they fell flat. Each had fallen into one of two areas, too condescending or of promising too much.

She had asked the Chairman of the Joint Chief of Staff if he had any candidates. He responded he had just the person she was looking for.

Jorge had been surprised to be called to a meeting with the Chairman of the Joint Chief of Staff.

He had been appraised that he was being considered to lead a project of personal interest to the new President and would be interviewed by her right after their meeting. Not much about the role was shared other than it would entail leading a team focused on exploring the solar system.

This pleased Jorge. His longtime friend and stiff competitor, Jerry Delaney had landed the assignment he had been seeking. He had not been aware of this opportunity and wasn't even sure he knew what it entailed.

"I wonder what my chances are at getting this assignment," he continued his musing. He hoped his knowledge about the solar system and space would help in getting through the interview.

He left the meeting with the Chairman and proceeded to the White House as instructed. The sun was getting close to the horizon when he entered the White House. He hoped the President would still hold the interview before going to lunch as scheduled.

Jorge looked up as the meeting room door opened. He stood up and gave the President a salute.

"I have never been greeted so formally. I am not sure how I should respond," Lacy commented.

"You should hire me to lead your team and I will salute you every time," Jorge replied with a slight smile.

"I believe I will. Just answer one question; Can you do this in the next four years," Lacy inquired?

"I don't make promises unless I can keep them. However, if it can possibly be done, I will do it. What is it that you want done," Jorge replied?

"I want a team to open up our solar system to exploration," Stacy replied.

She watched as Jorge took in the request. He seemed to be evaluating his options. Finally, he replied.

"I will put the US out in front of any progress of getting out and exploring the solar system. This is a race, and I will keep our team in the lead. I cannot promise the opening of the solar system, but I can promise we will be in the lead," Jorge replied.

He was not sure that his answer would be sufficient, but he would not over promise.

"Too hot, too cold, just right went through Lacy's mind before she declared, "You're hired."

I want this to be your team and I want it to deliver results. The details of the assignment are in this folder. All resources are at your disposal. At our next meeting please brief me on team member selection and the reason for your picks," President MacAdam said as the meeting came to a close.

As promised, Jorge called his wife to share the good news about his new job which he was not clear about and had yet to figure out.

This assignment will be the most challenging and perhaps the most important one in my career," Jorge thought to himself.

He realized that there were very few roles that would have him working with the President of the United States.

As he read through the material that he had been given he named the program "The Door." The briefing on the program was an eye opener.

"Are we really that close to achieving living matter transmission," was Jorge's question during the subsequent briefing by the Presidential Science advisor?

"That General, is what you are to determine and to accelerate to success," was the reply.

"You will lead a small team made up of a few scientists, analysts, and mathematical wizards. We have done a preliminary screening of potential team members."

We have lined up interviews with the top thinkers in the field. Your job is to select from among the candidates on the list and create the team you feel will lead to the goal of a quick success.

Jorge left the meeting with the list of candidates and had an interview schedule set up. He then began the interview process.

The choices had been tough to make but, in each case, Jorge got the mental signal, "this one is for the team, or no not this one."

The first series of interviews had been with the scientists directly involved with matter transmission. The early interviews had not gone well.

Jorge was disappointed by the initial interviews.

"These scientists are all still thinking theoretically and talking about what will happen in the future. I need one that is thinking about being successful tomorrow," Jorge had thought to himself.

He first conducted all the interviews that had been lined up in the US and Canada, his final interview took Jorge to England.

Jorge was zero for five in finding the right scientist as he went for this final interview. He had saved the husband-and-wife team of Tom and Linda to last.

"I don't know what I am going do if this last interview falls through," Jorge thought to himself as he stepped out of the Heathrow terminal and got into his cab.

Tom had grown up on the poor side of London. Both of his parents worked to make ends meet. He had been bored for most of his high school years but knew how to pass tests and get top grades. Those top grades got him into the University.

He was the first in his family to attend University. There he pursued a science curriculum but was bored with most of the topics. There just seemed to be nothing to provide the challenge he was looking for.

It was at the moment he was contemplating dropping out of the University when he met Linda. He was sitting at the end of the bar moping about and feeling sorry for himself when she offered to buy him a drink!

Tom had almost fallen off the stool.

Linda had seen Tom several times. His red hair was like a magnet to her. When she walked into the pub and saw him sitting at the end of the bar, she summoned all her courage and made the pass of her life by offering to buy him a drink.

His silence and stunned look made her think she had made a mistake. She turned in embarrassment to leave.

"Wait, Wait, yes, yes of course you can buy me a drink," Tom stammered as he recovered from his amazement.

"I can't let this beautiful creature escape from my presence," flashed through Tom's mind.

To have someone offer him a drink was unfathomable in his mind. To have this beauty make a pass at him threw him off his chair. A beer never tasted so good.

What followed was a romance that was to last a lifetime. Tom could not remember one word of their conversation on that first evening. For the rest of his life, he would sit and remember getting lost in Linda's eyes and wondering why she would want to have a drink with him!

Together they made a complete scientific team. Tom had a new purpose when Linda described her theory of living matter transmission.

The theory, mathematics, and physics associated with the topic were the ingredients needed to provide him a challenge.

The work he and Linda were doing limited their job market appeal. They landed several University based stipends and continued pursuing their matter transmission work. Several of their scientific papers on the topic of matter transmission were published and provided some meager additional income.

They spent almost ten years in their common pursuit. Ten years but it seemed like just yesterday to him.

He came to realize that the two of them had worked all this time and seemed on the verge of a breakthrough but were facing poverty because they were stuck on their work and needing a job.

"I feel like I am at the end of the bar again. Sitting and thinking that I was a failure. You came in and changed my life." Tom had commented to Linda.

"Are you looking for another offer of a free drink," Linda replied.

"I think we both need an offer for a free drink," Tom said as he gave her a kiss on the forehead.

That afternoon he got the call from the General. Tom had eagerly invited him over.

"We are on the verge. We have developed not only the theory but have defined the equipment needed to deliver our theory. If you build what we have designed, we will indeed be successful in transmitting living matter," he said excitedly during discussion with the General.

"It will be so much more personal, and our joint office is here at home and has all our analysis and information," Tom had replied when asked where they should meet.

Jorge made the trip to London and gone to Tom's house.

Jorge was now sitting in the kitchen of the Hughes's home in London. Tom had insisted that he come to dinner to do the interview. This was unusual for Jorge, but he accepted the invitation.

"These are the ones," had flashed through Jorge's mind as he listened to the energized manner in which Tom described the process and the quiet confidence Linda exuded as she provided the additional details.

"Who else do we need on the team," Jorge asked Tom and Linda?

"We need someone that can design and build the scanner that will disassemble the living matter at a molecular level at the transmission end and then recombine it at the receiving end.

We have the specifications for both pieces of equipment. We are sure they will work if we can get them built," Tom had replied.

Jorge looked down his candidates list. He concluded that he was dining with the two best candidates.

"I would like to offer both of you a role on The Door program.

Is there a chance one of you can participate in the interview of an Aaron Alton? He is the only one on my list that fits the profile you just described of having someone on the team that could get the equipment built," was Jorge's next statement.

"Yes of course, let us know the time and date and we will both participate," Linda spoke up.

"I hope you are going to cover the expenses. We are excited about the opportunity because we are essentially broke," she continued.

"This is wonderful. Don't worry, the project will cover all expenses as well as your salaries. I will send you the details on the salary and send you the time and date of Aaron's interview. We will also need to discuss the timing of your move to the Lakland airbase in San Antonio.

"What by the way is the salary offer you are making," Linda asked?

Both she and Tom looked at each other with beaming smiles when the General mentioned the salary each of them would receive.

They danced a jig together after the General got into the cab.

Together they would earn almost eight times their current combined income.

Jorge contacted Aaron Alton and arranged for an interview.

Jorge departed London the next day. He adjusted his return to San Antonio to go via Cincinnati, Ohio.

"Aaron is the opposite of Tom," flashed through Jorge's mind as he listened to Aaron's quiet, professional, and subdued responses.

"Yes, given the money, I can build an analyzer that will scan and capture the structure of every cell in the body. You say that you have the specifications for what the scanner must do. "When can I have access to them," was Aaron's reply to Jorge's pointed question?

"I would like to invite you to come to San Antonio to meet with several of The Door team members for a discussion on this topic," Jorge offered.

"Sure, that would be welcomed. I am currently at the end of a project and was looking for the next challenge." Aaron replied in a thoughtful manner.

He was as excited as he could possibly be. He had been bored to death with his current work at the University. He left the meeting and rushed home to tell his wife and kids about this new opportunity.

A few weeks later, Jorge, Tom, Linda, and Aaron got into the technology and the detailed specifications Linda and Tom had documented.

It was clear to Jorge that the three were technically and scientifically linked.

He listened politely but understood little. He was more focused on the dynamics of the three than trying to understand the technical aspects.

The conversation amongst the three was beyond Jorge's understanding.

He quickly positioned the three. Aaron's quiet low key attituded was a clear counterbalance to Tom's constant high energy enthusiasm and Linda was the pivot point and fulcrum for both of them.

He was please to think about the fact that Tom would be the fuel that would keep things hot.

"I have the core of my team. Now to round it out," Jorge thought to himself.

He was now looking to fill only two other roles. One was the role of planner and project manager. The other was the role of psychologist/psychiatrist.

Jacqueline Hazely, a petite, five foot, almost frail woman, turned out to have huge mental capacity. Her style was non-threatening but direct and firm. It was somewhat of a surprise to Jorge to find out her home was also in Cincinnati.

Jacque still had children in junior high and high school. She was very interested in the opportunity but made it clear it would need to be on a travel basis until the time she could get the family to agree to a move.

Jorge had immediately been drawn to her professional, direct, and effective communication style. She was the first on his list. He offered her a role on the spot, and she accepted.

Ryan McComber, the number one project manager on a long list of planners lived in Fort Wayne, Indiana. He would be the youngest member of the team. He had made the list because of his work on a website that had been delivered on time and had been a commercial success.

Their meeting took place in an Oyster Bar that Ryan had suggested.

Ryan was visually the opposite of the impression Jorge had gotten from his resume and their phone conversation. He sported a trim goatee and gave the visual impression of a rough and tumble type of person. His smooth conversational manners communicated a person who got along with everyone.

"You come highly recommended. Are you available for the job of a lifetime," Jorge opened their conversation?

"I am always looking for the job of a lifetime. "What part of my body do I have to give up," Ryan had replied?

Jorge figured that this sense of humor would later play well when managing a team of high energy people.

Ryan's children were young enough that he was willing to move the family to Texas so he could physically be part of the team.

A few weeks later the entire team was together for a barbeque in Jorge's backyard.

"Well, they seem to be getting along well," his wife commented to Jorge as they stood by the grill and looked at the table on the back patio and the people talking in an animated way.

"Yes, I am pleased with how they get along. They will need to make a major technical breakthrough. My job is to provide the resources to make it happen. If they fail, I fail," Jorge replied.

Chapter 2: The weak link

Elena had been hired to infiltrate "The Door" program. She had been in the spy business since her early years. Her Northern European, blond hair, blue eyes and her mother's beauty were the attributes that made it easy to attract the opposite gender. She knew from an early age that she was considered beautiful looking.

As she grew to be up and became a full grown woman she had observed many a man staring down her low-cut dress at her cleavage and eying her well-shaped slender legs.

She had learned to manipulate the men she associated with, and most had gone on to make fools of themselves. She had accidentally stumbled into her current role as a seductress.

Elena had leveraged this natural magnetism into a very lucrative business. This current assignment was by far the riskiest she had ever undertaken. It was also the most lucrative engagement. Because of the money she was being paid, she knew she had crossed over into the big league of spying.

Her benefactors had given her the backgrounds of all the known leaders of the US Door program. There had seemed to be no obvious weak link.

Her only hope and target was Colonel Sloan the security officer of the Door project. Of all the targets he was the one that should have been the most inaccessible.

After all he was the Chief Security Officer for the program!

However, he had separated from his wife and was currently out as newbie in the dating field.

Elena figured that it was the crack in the door that might allow her to get to the information she sought.

It was a daring move on Elena's part to pick him as her entry point.

It also turned out to be a brilliant move.

Her cover as a self-employed real-estate agent in San Jose, provided her with a rather good income but more importantly it provided the flexible hours she needed.

She had carefully followed the Colonel to learn of his social patterns. It became clear to her that some other people were following him as well. This sent up a warning light in her mind. She had competition but she did not know who it might be.

Nevertheless, she proceeded to make contact. She made her move to meet the Colonel at one of the night spots he periodically frequented.

Elena had made it as easy as possible for Phil to have her background checked. She had reviewed her past profile to make sure there were no obvious flags that would expose her as a spy.

She knew she had cleared the background check prior to her first date with him. Phil had proceeded slowly and carefully in establishing their relationship.

Elena woke up and contemplated the coming day.

"This has been one of my hardest assignments," she thought to herself as she looked across the bed at Phil.

This was her house, but Phil often slept over. He had his own home on the base.

Phil was sleeping peacefully. Periodic small snorts were his only sleep peculiarities.

Colonel Sylvester Sloan, know to his friends as Phil, was the Security Officer for the Door program. It was his job to ensure every participant in the program qualified for and maintained a Top Secrete Security Clearance. He was passionate about his job and made a point of digging deep into all personnel associated with the Door program.

He felt that he had finally found the woman of his dreams and she had cleared his security checks.

He was just an average looking guy but fancied himself a ladies' man. He was currently romancing Elena and working up to the point where he might propose to her.

Elena got out of bed and went to the kitchen to make herself a cup of coffee. She knew that Phil would soon follow her to the kitchen for his morning cup of coffee.

This past year she had pushed the relationship to a new level. Her employers wanted to know the progress of the US Door program. She surmised that there were other similar programs in several countries besides the program of her employer. From the tone of the inquiry coming from her employer it seemed apparent that things were not going too well in their program, and they were hoping to get some sort of lead from the US program.

"Something positive has happened in the US program," Elena thought to herself as she took her first sip of coffee.

"Phil has been much more ebullient than previous," she continued her musing.

She had learned about the countless mice that had lost their lives. She had not learned how but that the mice were dying but dying mice were indicators to her of a lack of success. Phil was very good at not divulging the details of the program.

However, she had learned that recently the mice were surviving. Surviving mice were to her a sign of success.

As soon as she had learned about mice surviving she had sent this information to her employers.

She felt Phil's arm go around her waist and then slide slowly up to her breasts.

She suppressed a shutter and leaned back into his arms as she was sure he was expecting her to.

"Good, morning beautiful," Phil said into her left ear.

"He at least brushed his teeth," Elena thought as she smelled his breath.

"Good Morning. Would you like a soft-boiled egg for breakfast," she replied.

"Yes, a couple of eggs and some coffee would be great. I am going out to get the paper," Phil said as he planted a kiss on her neck and let her go. He had enjoyed the embrace that he had given her. He walked out to get the paper.

Elena walked into the living room to watch Phil.

She observed the two men sitting in a light blue Toyota. It was clear they were on assignment to watch Phil.

She was sure that the black Chevy that was up the street about a block away had two men sitting in it and were assigned to watch her.

She was also aware of a watcher in the house next door.

She knew she was sitting at the center of a storm that might flare up at any moment. It was not a relaxing or comfortable spot to be in.

"What are you doing today," Phil asked a few minutes later as he sipped his coffee and scanned the paper.

"I have two houses to show," Elena was able to say truthfully.

She sold several homes a month and earned a significant income as a realtor.

"I wonder why I stay in the spy business," Elena thought to herself as she gave Phil a radiant smile. Then she thought of the millions that were accumulating in the offshore bank account.

"What are you up to today," Elena asked casually?

"I am going to see if the goat survives," Phil replied.

He did not see the surprised look on Elena's face.

"When did they move up to goats," Elena wondered to herself.

This was a significant increase in capability. She needed to get that information immediately to her employers.

"I am sure my benefactors will be very interested to hear that the program has moved from mice to goats," Elena thought. She wondered if there had been in-between animals that Phil had not mentioned.

She was not sure what it meant but it seemed that it must be a success. She would send in another report once Phil left for work.

"That reminds me. I am going by the bank today. "Do you need anything at the bank," Elena inquired?

She shared a safety deposit box with her handler. She would put her message into the safety deposit box. The message would be picked up after she put out her personal crest flag on the front door of her house. It seemed an archaic way to communicate but it was a way that stayed off the internet and the electronic media.

"No, I'm good. There is an ATM on base," Phil answered.

He was already thinking about his upcoming meeting with the General. He was getting a list of program participants that needed vetting.

He was keenly aware that they could not afford a leak about this program.

"I will be staying at the base for the next couple of days. It's going to get busy. How about planning a night out on Friday and then maybe we can go to the coast for the weekend," Phil suggested.

He would have loved to have Elena stay at his on base residence, but she had made it clear early on that she preferred the comfort of her own home. He had to agree her home was more modernly designed, well-furnished and more comfortable than his officers' quarters on the base.

"Friday and the weekend sound great. This week I have several houses to show. I will make arrangements for a place on the beach," Elena replied.

"This situation is perfect," she thought.

She watched Phil drive off. The light blue Toyota follow shortly after.

She looked up and down the street to see if the black car with the two who were observing her was still there. She was aware that they tailed her. This attention only heightened her awareness of the importance of the project. She now knew why she had been offered top dollar for her services.

She would need to make sure she survived so she could enjoy spending those dollars.

"This has to be my last job. I must get out before they move in and take me," Elena thought to herself.

She turned and walked back into the house to get ready for the day.

Next door the blinds moved slightly as the person inside stepped away from the window. His job was to keep track of the situation and at the right time erase any trail leading to his benefactors. The trail started in the house next door. He had bugged the home and was ablet keep track of what was occurring.

He went back and replayed the tape he had recorded of the conversations during the weekend and this morning. He would send this to the post office box address in Houston. He had no idea who got the information at that address, and it did not matter to him. For him it was just another clean up job.

He also reviewed the video taken of the vicinity around the house. The licenses of the observation vehicles made it clear that the Colonel and his lover were being observed by people in the FBI.

This was getting sticky and complicated. He was surprised that the situation had not unraveled.

Chapter 3: Lydia

Lydia sat quietly at the table. She knew something was wrong. She had fainted unexpectedly as she walked across the campus to class.

This was her last semester, and she was pushing hard to graduate on the Dean's list. She had attended the University of Tennessee on a full scholastic scholarship.

In her first year she had been active and had tried to be elected as class president. She had lost to an affable young man that she later dated a few times. She looked back at the election loss and was glad it had happened.

Her classes were harder than she had expected. She had to work ten times harder to maintain her grades then when she was in high school. In high school she had been a cheerleader on the football team, she had been active on the student council, and she had been class president. She had scored very high on her SAT and had been awarded a scholarship to U.T.

But she had not been ready for college! It required more from her than she had expected but she had stepped up and met the challenge. She was looking forward to graduation.

For the past month she had been feeling very tired. First, she thought it was just an unusually intense period of long study hours. But after her fainting spell, she was not sure.

Was she pregnant? She went over her recent hook ups and decided that was not possible.

She had come into the clinic where they had done an initial screening and had taken a series of blood samples. She had to look away and close her eyes when the nurse put the rubber strap around her arm and slowly pushed the huge needle into the vein in her arm. Then she looked back to watch the blood fill each vial.

This somehow fascinated her.

It had taken almost a week for the medical office to call her back.

"We would like you to go to the hospital for some additional tests. Do you have time this afternoon," the nurse at the other end of the phone had asked her?

"Yes, no problem," Lydia replied.

She had only one more test in psychology scheduled for the following day and she would be done. Done and if her psychology test went well, she would be at the top of her class.

She arrived at the hospital and walked directly to the check in counter.

"Yes, Miss Tabata, please got to booth three and the nurse will take the necessary information before you go to see your doctor," the grandmotherly volunteer informed her.

"I didn't know I was getting checked in," Lydia had replied.

"Oh, it doesn't matter what you get done here at the hospital, everyone gets checked in," had been the reply.

"Thanks for having brought in all the necessary information. Let me put this identifying band on your wrist. Then please wait there in the waiting area until an attendant can take you back," the nurse on the other side of the counter rattled off her standard speech in a monotone voice.

"Exactly where is the attendant taking me," Lydia asked still unsure what was going on?

"Let's see, you will be going to X-ray for a breast examination," had been the reply.

Lydia's inner alarm bells went off.

"I wish I had asked someone to come with me," flashed through her mind.

Then she gave a chuckle as she thought about the fact that in the past year, she had become a loner. For the first time in her life, she had not been part of the crowd. She had put everything into making her last year, her best year.

In fact, she now looked back and realized that her early years had been years of trying to be accepted. She had decided to become a psychologist because she wanted to understand herself.

Her time at the university and her curriculum had changed her totally.

"You have really matured," her mother had told her during the family Christmas gathering. "I am so proud of you."

Her father had told her the same thing and had offered to pay whatever it cost for her to become a psychologist.

"Lydia, Lydia Tabata," a bearded young man called out.

He was standing behind a wheelchair calling out her name.

"Yes, that's me," Lydia replied as she was pulled back into the present.

Lydia knew immediately that her looks were affecting her wheelchair pusher. He had blushed when she had looked at him. She wished that the opposite sex didn't always get distracted by her looks. It was a constant occurrence to be either ogled or have guys turn away trying not to stare and other guys hitting on her

The fact that the attendant was taking her to get a breast X-ray seemed to have totally locked up his tongue.

They arrived in the check-in desk where she got out of the wheelchair and presented her papers.

When she turned to sit down, she saw that the wheelchair was gone.

She tried to recall her last breast X-ray only a couple of years ago.

Finally, she was taken in and had each breast X-rayed from several angles. This was more thorough than she remembered from before. She knew better than to ask the X-ray technician why, but she did anyway.

"Your doctor is here and asked me to send your file immediately up to her. She will be seeing you shortly," the technician had informed her as she evaded giving a direct reply.

This time her wheelchair attendant was a young black lady whose smile and chatter eased Lydia's apprehension.

"I am Dr. Lisa Meyerhof. I am an oncologist," a very young blond lady introduced herself.

Lydia thought she looked too young to be a practicing specialist.

"Pleased to meet you," Lydia replied but a chill ran up the back of her neck.

"I will get right to the point. You are in the advanced stages of breast cancer. It has metastasized and is spreading throughout your body. I am surprised you did not get some sort of early warning," Dr. Meyerhof rapidly delivered her message.

It was clear she was uncomfortable in delivering her message.

"Do you mind if I take a minute to let my mind absorb this," Lydia replied as she sat back in the chair.

"So, what are my chances and treatment," Lydia inquired?

"I am sorry to be the one that tells you that at this stage, even with chemotherapy, there is only a 10% chance of survival beyond six months" Dr. Meyerhof replied.

"Wow, you certainly know how to deflate someone's hopes," Lydia replied

"I am sorry. I just don't know how to soften the message," was the reply.

"No, I am not referring to you personally. I was just thinking about my final test tomorrow and the two job offers I am still being courted for," Lydia replied.

She now saw her future take a very different direction then she had ever imagined.

"What do you recommend," Lydia inquired.

"I reviewed your case with the head of the department. The probability of survival beyond six months is extremely low. He suggests you get your affairs in order and enjoy the remaining time as best as you can. We will provide any medication for pain or nausea, but we don't feel any of the more aggressive treatments are appropriate in your case.

The department head did mention that a US Air Force colleague has put out a request for volunteers willing to participate in a high-risk break through project. It has nothing to do with a cure. It has to do with the high risk of death the volunteer will face during the project," Dr. Meyerhof replied.

"So, I am given a death sentence and an offer to participate in a project that may kill me. What additional twist can be put on this knife that is stabbing me," Lydia asked in a fatalistic tone?

"I am sorry. I didn't want to mention this, but I was told to do so. I feel so bad about your case," Dr. Meyerhof said as she lost her composure and began to cry.

Lydia watched the tears run down her doctor's cheek.

"It's OK," Lydia said as she patted the doctor on her back.

"My mind is racing, and I am just a little disoriented. Tell your boss that I want to hear more about this volunteer thing with the Air Force. I am going to leave now and focus on my test for tomorrow. Who should I call," Lydia asked as she made up her mind to leave?

She did not wait for the wheelchair transport out of the hospital but walk briskly away from the hospital. She went straight to her favorite place along the Tennessee River for a cup of coffee.

She needed time to think. Time! She wanted time to live!

She was still blankly looking out at the river when her phone vibrated on the table.

"Hello, this is Lydia," she said.

"Hello Lydia, I am very sorry to hear about your situation. I am General Jorge Martinez with the US Air Force. "Is this a good time to talk," the general inquired?

Jorge had immediately reacted when he had been given Lydia's name. He wanted to touch base with his first candidate as soon as possible.

"Well, I don't know if this is a good time or not. However, since we are talking, please tell me more about this high-risk opportunity you are extending to those of us who have received a death sentence," Lydia said a little sarcastically.

She really wanted to hit someone or something.

"Let's plan to talk tomorrow evening. May I take you out to dinner? I will explain everything in detail at that time," Jorge proposed.

"Ok" Lydia replied

"Good, Good, I will text you the details. We will pick you up outside your dorm at six. Will that work," Jorge inquired?

"Sure," was Lydia's simple reply.

How did he know she lived in the dorm? He had not asked which dorm but said he would meet her at the curb.

"Who were these people?"

"Well, that is the last test I take maybe for the rest of my life," Lydia thought to herself the next day as she walked out of the test room.

The rest of her life! This next horizon suddenly seemed much too close.

She felt like she had aced her last test.

The grey drizzly day that met her as she stepped outside fit her current mood.

She was trying to decide how she was going to tell her family. She had already decided to wait until she got home so she could deliver the message in person.

She walked aimlessly for the next few hours. Later she would not remember anything she might have been thinking about. It was a completely blank period of time.

At six she walked out to the curb. She was not surprised to see a car blink its headlights at her. The back door opened, and a pleasant, mild-mannered man stepped out. He was not in uniform, but she could tell by his looks that he was definitely in the military.

"Lydia, I am Jorge Martinez, General in the Air Force. I am very pleased to meet you," Jorge said as he extended his hand.

She was just as beautiful in person as her pictures Jorge thought to himself.

"Lydia," she replied shaking his hand.

"Would Calgain's On the River be a good place for you," Jorge inquired?

"Yes, that would be a great place to celebrate my last day here," Lydia replied.

She liked the choice. She had eaten there once before when her parents first brought her to school.

This visit would complete the circle.

After listening to the General's description of the project she had agreed to participate in the matter transmission program. To be among the first at something before she died was now her final goal.

When she looked into the mirror, she did not see a dying person. She still had all of her long black hair. Her figure still turned heads. But the cancer had spread throughout her body and had penetrated to the bone marrow. In the next few months, the decay would be fast and final.

All she had noticed at this point was the fatigue.

She returned home to visit with her parents before going on to Lakland Air Force base in San Antonio.

She waited until after dinner on the first evening before saying anything. Then when they were finally sitting in the family room, she told her parents and her brother.

Her parents were devastated. Her mother began to cry, and her father had that long sad face he put on when something he could not change bothered him. He held her mother but said nothing. Tears were brimming in his eyes and his chin was quivering.

Her younger brother Jarret, the high school jock, stomped out of the room.

Lydia went after him and found him in his room crying.

He had not wanted to break down if front of her.

She held him and said, "It's alright. I'm frightened but not afraid."

"It's just not fair, not fair," he said through his tears.

The week passed fairly quickly. She visited with her old friends in the neighborhood. She had gone out a couple of times with friends to eat. The rest of the time she spent with the family, did a little gardening, and spent time with her brother.

He was taking it the hardest.

Then it was time to leave. The family took her to the Chattanooga airport.

"The General sent me round trip tickets to San Antonio. I hope I can return but if not, I want you to know I am proud of you," she told her brother.

She gave her tearful mother a hug and then hugged her father.

"Well, we are all proud of you and we love you," her father said just loud enough for them all to hear.

The flight was routed through Atlanta and then directly to San Antonio. She was pleased to have someone meet her and take her to her hotel. She was put into a popular hotel suite and was immediately impressed with the room. There was a vase of flowers and a note from the General welcoming her.

The General had told her she officially had a job with the Door program and that all her expenses would be paid by the program. He told her to overspend on everything!

"I am to pick you up in the morning at nine to take you to the base," the airman informed her.

The next day she was taken to building fifty-one. Lydia smiled as the number sent the word aliens to her brain.

She was taken to a room with a table and four chairs. She had taken the chair facing the door. It was only a few minutes later when the door opened, and Lydia looked up.

"Hello Lydia, it is good to see you again. How was the visit with the family," Jorge said as he sat down across the table?

"It was a good visit but a hard one for everyone in the family," she replied as she looked steadily at the General.

She was not familiar with military ranks but the three stars on the shoulders of the uniform made it clear Jorge was indeed a General.

Jorge was surprised at her calm beauty and self-assurance and thought, "life is not fair."

"I wanted to hear from you and make sure you understand the risk you will be taking if you go through with this trial," Jorge said as he moved around the table.

He pulled out the chair next to Lydia and sat down and sat facing her.

He took her hand and asked, "What if the test is a failure?"

"If it fails, at least I was taking positive action to achieve something, not just sitting around waiting to die," Lydia replied as she looked steadily into the General's eyes.

She could see genuine concern. She made an immediate connection with him.

"Good, you are especially brave but if you change your mind, let me know. There is no shame in being afraid," Jorge replied as he gave her a pat on the back of her hand, followed by a light squeeze.

"There are three of you who have volunteered. What order do you want," Jorge asked as he stood and got ready to leave?

"I prefer to be the first. I don't think I am brave enough to be second or third," Lydia replied.

If something went wrong with an early trial, she was not sure she would be able to go through with it.

"I can't promise it at this moment but be assured, I have heard your request," Jorge replied.

Chapter 4: Darian

Darian was replaying his departure from home. His mother was in tears as she hugged him. His whole family at the airport departure gate with him. The tears and sad looks as the family waited for the boarding call. His two younger brothers constantly looking down and periodically looking back at him. His Dad with his arm around his shoulders. "Just know how proud I am of you. And always remember that everyone loves you," his Dad had said quietly.

That had brought tears to Darian's eyes. He wished he had done something to earn his Dad's pride.

It now brought tears to his eyes again as he recalled the moment.

He was glad his three girlfriends had not been allowed to come to the gate. It still surprised him that the three knew about each other but had put up with his three timing ways. He had believed he was managing the three, so they did not know about each other.

He was the last to board the plane to San Antonio. The folks on board had taken notice and one of the older men had commented about being deployed to fight in Iraq and said that it was hard to leave his family as well.

Darian wished he had been as brave as the guy talking to him and at least have done what the speaker had been willing to do.

He put his accomplishments at close to a zero.

On his arrival in San Antonio, he had been met by an airman with a van and escorted to the hotel. It had a large interior open area with a coy pond and a restaurant breakfast area. He was impressed as he watched the elevator rise up toward the interior roof suite.

He had been a poor student for enough years that it was comforting to know that he did not have to pay. He planned to enjoy his free breakfasts and he hoped lunches and dinners as well.

At this point he was clueless how what he had volunteered to be a participant in would work or what was immediately ahead of him.

He figured that time might be limited for him, but good times would not be ignored.

The next few days passed quickly. He was interviewed and he guessed that he had been assessed as to his mental condition.

He got along well with the person assessing his mental state.

"Well does this dying guy have a chance to participate in the program or are you going to fail me," he joked with Jacque as he had come to call his analyst.

He had spent several days being interviewed.

Jacqueline had introduced herself as the psychologist of the project. He was surprised that such a petite body could exude such confidence and control.

He noted that she was also very good looking, and he tried flirting with her but either he was too young for her, or she was just not interested is some dude who was dying.

As it turned out he was impressed with her thoroughness, keen insight, and her focus on getting him to share very personal feelings.

He relaxed and enjoyed the mental checks and other questions she was asking him. She was fun to joke with and he was confident enough to joke with her.

Darian had been sitting in the meeting room going through all the recent events when he suddenly realized that some high-level brass was standing in front of him.

"Good heavens do all good-looking young people end up with incurable diseases," Jorge thought as he sat down and introduced himself to the young man across the table.

Darian was not sure what the protocol was for meeting with some sort of top military brass.

So, he stood up and introduced himself.

"Hi, I am Darian, but I missed your name," he said as he stood up and extended his hand.

"Hello, Darian, I am Jorge Martinez. I am in charge of this project. I wanted to meet with you and talk to you directly before proceeding," Jorge said.

"Tell me a little about yourself and the reason you volunteered," Jorge continued.

"The news about my melanoma and the fact that it was in its later stage when it was found threw me. It was the last thing I or my family expected. They are taking it harder than I am.

The death sentence threw me for a loop.

I remembered my Dad often saying, "We all will die someday."

I had always thought that would be when I grew old like him," Darian rattled off.

He continued when he realized the General was only shaking his head in agreement but not saying a word.

"Life was good at Penn State. I was majoring in business. It was a breeze. I spent more time partying than studying and I was still carrying an OK grade point average.

As I said, life seemed good.

Then on one of my trips home, my mom scheduled a checkup with our family doctor.

He looked at three different spots on my back, my side and one on my arm.

I should have known something bad was up when he sent me to an oncologist.

They took samples and they all came back positive. What was worse was that the blood test showed that the cancer had spread.

The doctor suggested that chemotherapy and radiation therapy might buy me a few extra months but predicted that in either case I had about six months to live.

That doctor must know you personally because he knew you were looking for some volunteers," Darian finished.

"Yes, Doctor Snyder is a family friend.

Why did you take him up on the suggestion to volunteer for this project," Jorge inquired?

"I realized I had been playing for years. I was not really focused on accomplishing anything other than having fun. I thought I had a lifetime to accomplish something. Then WHAM, my life is over, and my accomplishment score is ....a big fat ZERO.

Wouldn't you volunteer if this was the only chance you would get in your life to make a big score," Darian replied?

"You realize you will be among the first to see if this technology is good enough for humans. It has worked on smaller animals, but we don't know how it will affect a person," Jorge said as he kept a steady gaze on Darian.

"Yeh, the red headed guy, I believe Tom is his name, mentioned that and so did Dr. Jacque.

Tom was selling me on the idea and mentioned his latest success with a pig.

Dr. J was testing me mentally to see if I was mentally balanced.

In either case I figure if a pig made it OK and still thought they were pigs, I would give it a try," Darian said with a smile.

"OK, do you want to be first or second," Jorge countered as he gave Darian a smile.

This was his way of checking how each individual was thinking about the test.

"Heck that's a no brainer. In this case second puts one human before me and I will know whether to be crying or laughing when I either go in willingly or you drag me in as I scream bloody murder," Darian replied with a chuckle.

He was watching the General as intensely as he saw General was watching him.

Darian loved mind games.

"Thank you. It was good to talk with you. We will be working together and will see each other often. I will let you know the order in the next day or so. I have one more interview to go," Jorge said as he got up and opened the door to leave.

Darian was just looking around to see what to do next when Dr. J entered.

"We are all gathering for dinner at a Mexican restaurant. Would you care to join us," she asked?

She could see Darian's macho kick in as he seemed to puff up his chest.

"Finally," Darian thought to himself.

"Yes, that would be great. How do I get there," he asked?

Jackie mentally smiled to herself.

"They are so easy," she thought as he agreed and smiled at her.

She let him know that he would be escorted there by one of the drivers.

Chapter 5: Joe

Joe was born on a ranch about ten miles from the town of Canadian, the seat of Hemphill County, Texas. The population for the county was maybe three thousand people.

This was the home of the Canadian High School Wildcat football team. High school football was a big local past time in the fall. Since the school had so few eligible young men Joe had been required to play. It was not his personal interest but there were so few players that he felt obliged. He was a loner, not a team player. With his height, long arms, and sure hands he was a star back known for making the impossible catch.

He became a star player.

Joe's personal goal had been to get out of Canadian. He worked hard to keep his grades at the top of his class and had been pleasantly surprised to get several acceptance to three universities, He chose to go to Texas A&M and enjoyed the four years leading up to his Engineering degree. He worked hard, got top grades. He was a regular on the football team and enjoyed more partying than he cared to think about.

Inherently shy, he did not seek out a girlfriend, but many girls were friendly. He did not think himself handsome, but he had been told he looked like a real cowboy. He guessed this meant he was ruggedly handsome.

He had interviewed several big companies and had received job offers.

This was the good news.

The hiring companies wanted him to take a physical. This is when he received the really bad news.

He was in the late stages of acute myelogenous leukemia. This he learned was a death sentence.

He had thought his fatigue was due to putting in so many study hours.

Now he knew the real reason.

"I am sorry to be the bearer of such bad news. I am friends with a General in the Air Force. He is looking for volunteers in a special project. Your condition and intelligence makes you a perfect candidate for the project," the doctor informed him.

"That is actually welcome news. I don't believe the other job offers I am currently holding mean much anymore," Joe had replied.

He had wanted to leave Canadian.

He just never thought he would need to be dying to do so.

He chuckled to himself. Really sick humor.

He chuckled again.

"Sure, call your friend and tell him he has his human guinea pig," Joe replied.

His doctor made the call. He handed the phone to Joe and the next thing Joe knew he was talking to a General Jorge Martinez.

He seemed like a good guy.

"I would like to come up and meet with you. Is there a good restaurant in Canadian," Jorge inquired?

"Well, there are a few places. The Corral is one of the popular places," Joe had replied.

"However, I know my Dad well enough that he will want you to come out to the ranch and eat one of his grilled steaks," Joe continued.

His Dad hated to go out to eat and Joe was not going to meet with the General without his Dad.

Joe's mother had died when he was about six years old. He knew what she looked like because his Dad had shown him her picture often and he always mentioned her at all the events they had.

His Dad had raised him to be honest, determined, and independent.

Joe was not sure how his Dad would take the news about his cancer.

Joe came home to Canadian. He was picked up at the airport by both his Dad and Uncle Ted.

Uncle Ted was like a second father. He had lived at the ranch for as long Joe could remember. He was not actually Joe's uncle, but he had always been called that.

After Uncle Ted's welcome home dinner, they were all sitting out on the veranda watching he sunset when he shared the bad news.

"Son, I am sorry for your condition, and I want you to know how much joy you have been for me. I am so very proud of you," his Dad said when Joe broke the news.

He was as stoic as always, but Joe saw that he had to dry some tears from his eyes.

Uncle Ted had been present during this interchange and walked off the veranda without saying a word. Joe watched as he walked out to the old oak tree that still held the swing Joe had played on.

Uncle Ted sat there for the next hour just slowly swinging back and forth.

The General arrived the next day.

"Well, I am glad you found the ranch," Joe said as he greeted the General.

"Hello, I am General Jorge Martinez of the US Air Force," Jorge said in a formal tone.

This young man seemed to be on the serious side. The white Stetson hat made him look the part of the cowboy Jorge had expected.

"General, I am honored you took the time to come out. This is my Dad, Trey and the guy at the grill is Uncle Ted. Most folks just call me Joe," Joe made the introductions in a slow distinct manner and almost gave a salute.

He liked the tone and feel of the General.

"Hello General, thanks for taking my offer for a steak and drink here at the ranch. If you need to talk to Joe in private Ted and I will take a ride out on the range," Trey said as he extended his hand for a handshake.

"I am pleased to meet you. This is a sad time but one that offers Joe the opportunity to lead the way in the implementation of a technology that will transform mankind.

No, you won't need to go on any ride. I will only ask for your word that anything you learn will stay on this ranch," Jorge replied.

He could feel the pride and the strength of both Joe and his father.

"I am a city boy from Mexico, City. However, I spent a lot of time on my grandparents' cattle ranch when I was growing up. Their ranch was in Aguascalientes. This is one of the states of Mexico almost at the center of the country.

They farmed and raised cattle. They taught my sister and I to milk the cows, clean the barn and take care of the horses. I remember it as a simple and blessed time in my life," Jorge continued his introduction.

He wanted to put Trey at ease if he could.

"Well, we have a great garden, a couple of milk cows, some goats and sheep and a couple of dogs.

This is all thanks to Uncle Ted. I would have thrown in the towel on all the work that they take," Trey replied.

He liked Jorge almost immediately. He could tell that the General had a good heart.

"Come on let's eat before Uncle Ted burns the steaks," Trey beckoned as he turned and walked up onto the veranda.

"Tell me something about yourself and why you accepted my offer to participate in this program," Jorge inquired a moment later as he put a piece of steak in his mouth.

"Well, I figured this would be the quickest way to make a significant contribution. I don't have the luxury of time to work long and hard to do it," Joe replied.

It had not taken him long to realize that all the great jobs that had been offered would never come to be.

"The project you have volunteered for is about matter transfer. My team has successfully and rigorously tested this transmit and receive technology. I think we are the only ones in the world that have successfully achieved this ability with living matter," Jorge started into his explanation.

"Are you talking about matter transmission," Joe asked?

This was quite different than what he had though the experiment would be.

"Yes, we began with mice. We went through hundreds of them before we had a breakthrough. Since the first successful transmission of a mouse, we have transmitted rats, rabbits, goats, sheep and finally pigs," Jorge continued between bites of steak.

This was the first time Jorge had been given the chance to discuss the project in its entirety. He was surprised how easy it was to talk to the three.

The grilled asparagus was delicious. He was having a hard time focusing on the discussion about the project.

"By the way Uncle Ted, this is a great steak and I really like the grilled vegetables," Jorge said as he took a minute to engage the rest of the family.

The remainder of the baked potato was now getting his attention.

"Well, it all starts with the good meat from one of our cows. I just add salt, olive oil, some garlic and pepper. The grill does the rest. The vegetables all come from my garden. I grill them with a dab of coconut oil," Ted responded quietly but his face beamed with the praise.

"Well, I will be interested in getting some of these cattle delivered to San Jose so my team and I can enjoy this treat more often," Jorge responded.

"We would be glad to sell to the base," Trey replied quietly.

"So, you are recruiting human guinea pigs to be transmitted," Joe brought the conversation back to his initial question.

"Yes, there are three volunteers, there are three tests scheduled. You will be one of the three. I have already interviewed the other two. Are you still interested," Jorge inquired?

"Sure, I don't really have many other choices. It is either this or listen to Uncle Ted's stories for the next six months," Joe said with a smile.

"Hey, I tell good stories," Ted said defensively.

"Do you have a preference as to the order of your test," Jorge inquired?

"You choose the order. It sounds like you have some doubt about the success of the tests.

Don't worry, I won't cut and run if the tests are going bad or we come out thinking like pigs," Joe said with a lazy smile on his face.

He did hope for success for the sake of the other two, but he knew he would not back down.

"We have the spare room ready for tonight. Ted fixes a great breakfast. Will you accept the offer to stay here tonight," Trey inquired?

He had waited to make the offer until he was sure he liked the General.

"Thank you, yes I will accept the offer," Jorge replied after pausing to think for a minute.

He really enjoyed being with a family that worked so well together. It would be so much better than trying to find a hotel.

"In that case, can I get a ride with you tomorrow," Joe asked?

He figured this would give him a clean, fast break.

His Dad was taking the situation hard. He was stoic as ever, but Joe knew his Dad because he knew himself.

"It would be great to have some company on the way back," Jorge responded.

He sensed Joe was asking for help.

The next morning, after breakfast, Joe put his suitcase into the trunk of the black car.

"Here is a package of those steaks you liked so well. They are already seasoned. Just put them on the grill. Just don't overcook them," Ted said handing Jorge a small cooler.

"Well, thank you so much. I am sure my wife will love them," Jorge responded as he placed the cooler in the back seat of the car.

Joe gave a hug to both his Dad and Ted and got into the car.

"Remember son, Ted, your mother and I are proud of you," Trey said through Jorge's open window.

"I thought your mother passed away when you were young," Jorge said as they drove down the lane.

"She did but Dad brings her to every major event," Joe replied.

About an hour later Joe looked across at Jorge.

"There is a car following us," he said

"Yes, it is. I don't get to go anywhere by myself. I am sure those guys slept in their car at the end of the road leading to your ranch," Jorge replied.

He was impressed with the sense of presence Joe had.

"Why don't we stop early and buy them some lunch," Jorge suggested.

"Sounds fair to me," Joe replied.

The rest of the drive to San Antonio went without any problems. They stopped a couple of more times on the way to get a bite or a bio break.

"I will drop you off at the hotel. We have rented the entire top floor. There are guards posted at every entry or exit point," Jorge said as they entered the San Jose city limits.

Chapter 6: The Program

Three D printers had started the revolution in manufacturing. This revolution, still in its early stages, threatened the order of manufacturing. It could be a tremendous boon to mankind but the transition to this new world was potentially devastating to the manufacturing world order.

Matter transmission or perhaps better stated, microscopic production instruction transmission and receiver controlled recombination was the next step to the three D technique.

Jorge led a team with representation from the US, Great Britain, Canada, Germany and Italy and the remaining members of the EU. He was aware of similar teams in Israel, Brazil, China, India, and Japan.

The US's top-secret operation was secluded at the Lakland Air Force base in San Antonio, Texas. This location provided the space and was secluded enough to provide the level of security desired for the program.

Several variants of the mater transmission concept had come into existence almost at the same time.

57

Jorge knew that the Israeli and Brazilian approach was similar to his team's approach.

The Chinese and Indian approaches were similar to each other but very different from his team's approach.

As far as Jorge's and the US's intelligence could tell his team was technically in the lead.

"I'm not sure about our technical lead. Our guys would probably be afraid to tell us if we were behind.

All I know is that we are on a roll and making solid step by validated step progress," Jorge thought to himself.

All sides were trying to spy on each other.

The US was not shy about its spying, but it did not compare to the super aggressive Chinese spying activities.

Jorge understood the aggressiveness of the Chinese. To prevent any of his competitors from hacking into the Door's scientific results, all of the project's material and documents were kept in offline computers.

There were three physically separate independent computer systems. Information going from one system to another was kept to a minimum. Every file making the move from one system to another went through "scrubbers" designed to find any kernel of a spy code.

This off-line, three level computer security proved to be exactly what was required. They had already detected a break at the top level and installed a full metal wall around the computer room to prevent remote sensing of the computer electronics.

Jorge made sure everyone followed the three-level information storage protocol and had IT schedule weekly health checks of the system and procedures.

The transmit-receive equipment was the heart of the program. The ability to scan the subject to be transmitted at the microscopic level and then to be able to reconstitute the subject at a microscopic level utilizing material at the receiving end seemed incomprehensible but it worked.

Aaron designed and built the transmit-receive equipment as Linda had specified. He had been surprised at the thoroughness and exactness of Linda's design. His discussions with Linda and Tom convinced him they knew what they were doing.

"She may not be able to knit a stitch, but she certainly knows how to design equipment," Aaron thought to himself.

Even so Aaron remained somewhat skeptical.

Then the real testing began. The equipment seemed to operate as intended but the mice were dying or not appearing at the receiver end. The transmit system scanned and absorbed the transmit material and transformed it into part of the transmission energy. The receive end was working but what came through was disgusting.

Many mice saw their demise.

The breakthrough had come when Tom made what was supposed to be a monumental mistake. He had set the controls 180 degrees opposite to the settings he and Linda had calculated.

Tom got the first living mouse through.

Jorge was not so sure about it being a mistake. The exactness of the mistake gave it away.

Tom had done this on purpose.

Tom and Linda were working together when Tom supposedly accidentally reversed polarity on the matter transmission signal as he attempted to send the 1000th mouse through the system.

This was the lucky mouse.

The other nine hundred and ninety-nine had died on the spot or in route to Linda.

Most came out as disgusting little blobs of quivering matter.

"It's about time I do something different if I expect a different result," Tom thought to himself.

Linda's excited reaction when the mouse appeared on the receiving pad was, "I have a mouse, I have a mouse, oh my god, I have a mouse."

Jorge had monitored the subsequent progress from mouse to rat, to rabbit, to goat, to sheep and then to pigs.

The matter transmitter had grown in size and power requirement. The biggest part of the increasing power requirement was satisfied by the matter conversion to energy, which drove the matter being transmitted.

It was this self-amplification of the energy that made the program feasible.

Jorge immediately recognized that this specific feature would make the Door program a success.

Each successful transmission was greeted by Linda with; "I have a mouse."

This was the case even when she had the pig, but the mouse had earned its place in her hall of fame.

Then it was time to try it on a human. Three trials, with three young and still healthy individuals, was on the docket.

"Well, it is now time to try it on a human. How shall we proceed," Jorge posed the question to the team sitting around the meeting room table?

Phil was a member of the team and responsible for security. He had vetted every person on the team and felt he knew each almost as well as he knew himself.

"The three people you recruited are here and have signed all the legal paperwork," Phil responded.

"Our three terminally ill recruits have spent the last month undergoing every imaginable test in preparation for this event. It has been stressful for them, but they are still willing to take the risk," Linda replied.

The criteria for the first human subjects had been debated for some time. A terminally ill person made sense.

Jacqueline had pointed out that age could make quite a difference and using younger subjects would be better for the effort. She now felt a little guilty that her recommendation may have been what had gotten these recruits in the situation they now found themselves.

That these young recruits were willing to take such a risk spoke volumes about the principles by which they had been raised.

"How would I feel if they were my kids," she thought to herself?

The three subjects had been moved to the base, to the officer's housing area. This more secure location provided a means of isolating them from any external threat.

They had each undergone what seemed an impossible number of tests. A series of interviews, questions and specific mental tests had also been done. The goal was to be able to compare the early information to the information they would provide after the transmission.

The entire team was betting on success. They could not in good conscience participate if they felt the transmission would fail.

"Well after the rabbits, each subsequent transmission has been successful. In fact, the animals seem to come out in better shape than when they go in," Aaron added.

Aaron had moved on from being the system designer to being their chief data analyst. He had run every analysis and test on the transmitted subjects he could possibly do without dissecting them.

The first few rats and rabbits had in fact been dissected for more detailed examination. He had gone back multiple times when his analysis showed the animals healthier on the receiving end versus the transmission end. One of the pigs, for instance, had lost three scars that were originally on his snout.

The discussion had been on the accuracy of the brain in the receiving recombination.

Linda and Tom participated in the interviews. It was clear to them that the subjects saw this as their last contribution before they died. It was hard to see such young people face such a hard fact.

"Each participant understands the risk. This is their only chance to make a contribution before they die. My biggest concern is whether they will come out being the same person mentally as when they began," Tom continued.

He was most concerned about the accuracy of transformation of the brain and the retention of memories.

"We are who we think we are. We are our brains. When they come out the receiving end I want them to be the persons who went into the transmission chamber," Tom worried to himself.

"I have interviewed each of the subjects. Each passes our stability and other psychological tests, and each wants to go through the process. Tom is right, the subjects see this as their only chance to put meaning into their life," Jacqueline said in a quiet tone.

"There are two males and one female subject. You have all met them. They are all suffering the final stages of their fight against cancer. Each has a different cancer. Darian has melanoma, Joe, our cowboy, has acute myelogenous leukemia and the Lydia has advanced breast cancer."

Jacque, their psychiatrist, and psychologist did double duty.

She was dealing with the fact that transmission was really a misnomer. In fact, the manner of transmission bothered her. One error and the subject died. There was no recovery.

She was concerned that their brilliant but too flippant red haired mad scientist didn't take this seriously enough.

Why would he have reversed the polarity on the transmission unit when there was no scientific basis to do so?

What else might he and Linda have missed?

Tom on the other hand used the old quote, "What is crazier than doing the same thing over and over and expecting a different outcome," he responded to defend himself.

In fact, he thought, "How could I have killed nine hundred and ninety-nine mice before trying something different?"

Jacque just felt guilty for telling the three that everything would turn out alright when in fact she had no clue if it would.

A separate monitoring and care facility was set up at the base hospital. One entire floor of the facility was isolated and dedicated to the tests each went through in preparation and would go through again once successful transmission had been achieved.

The facility was remodeled to resemble a resort motel versus the traditional hospital.

Each of the subjects would spend a great deal of time undergoing the pre-transmission test and then the post-transmission test.

Jorge thought about this and stressed the fact that success was the goal and to fully utilize the facilities as intended would be success.

The technology was one of controlled destruction and reconstruction. The scanner was much like a Computed Tomography (CT) scanner. Only it was much more sophisticated and precise. The beam sliced through each and every atom in the body, gathering the characteristic and placement of every atom as it destroyed it.

A huge burst of energy occurred in the chamber holding the subject to be transported. This energy was utilized to power the transmission. The transmission sent the majority of the power in its beam to the receiving chamber.

The receiving end received the atom-by-atom reconstruction instructions and the accompanying energy. It utilized atoms from its own material chamber and recombined the atoms as instructed by the transmission signal.

The incoming energy provided ninety percent of the energy need and the reconstruction happened at almost lightning speed. The super high-speed camera monitoring the chamber recorded the assembly of atoms taking the form of the transmitted subject.

To the human eye it appeared the subject winked into existence. When analyzed in slow motion it appeared that the reconstruction was being done slowly, methodically and with a precision never before achieved.

The transmission began at the head and the reconstruction began at the same point. When the images of the two chambers were monitored sided by side it seemed as if the transfer from one location to the other was occurring in a synchronous manner. This was of course not the case. The camera speed was several magnitudes slower in the speed of capturing the image versus transmit and receive speed.

Those who were shy would be embarrassed. The subject began the process in the nude and came out the same way.

"When are we scheduling the first test," Jorge inquired?

"Three trials are planned. There will be two weeks between each test. This will allow time for analysis and making any adjustments that the team decides are necessary," Ryan took over as he projected the critical path timeline on the screen.

He had worked with the entire team to create the project timeline and the exact schedule of each event.

"It's good to see we are ready and organized for the first three transmissions.

After the first transmission success, let's take a first cut on the plan beyond these initial trials. I want us to be ready to go into full production of these units," Jorge informed the team.

"Let's plan on dinner together at our favorite Mexican restaurant," he said as he got up to leave. We have kept our recruits isolated from each other for the past month. Let's make sure our three recruits make it there tonight and get a chance to meet each other," Jorge said as the meeting broke up.

The gathering at the restaurant was the first time the three candidates had the opportunity to meet each other.

When Joe walked in, he was set back by Lydia's good looks. He had seen her at the hospital in passing but did not realize that she was one of the volunteers.

Darian, who was sitting next to Lydia and talking to her, also caught Joe's attention. He also felt physically outclassed by Darian's good looks.

"Well, it's good that we don't have to worry about who gets whom since we will all soon be dead," he thought as he gave Lydia a tip of his hat and a wink as he sat down across from her.

Lydia had immediately pegged Darian as a player. He was good looking, and he knew it. Not her type, she mentally made a note to that effect.

Joe on the other hand was just ruggedly good looking and seemed bashful except for his wink at the end. She liked him immediately. Too bad they had not met under better circumstances.

"Does everyone have a drink of choice? Let's toast to the success of the next three transmissions and to the brave volunteers willing to take a chance on Tom and Linda," Jorge said as he lifted his Corona and began clinking glasses and bottles.

"I will now announce the order of transmission," Jorge continued after everyone had put down their drinks.

Chapter 7: Preparation

The following day, Lydia, Darian, and Joe met together with the rest of the team. They were briefed on the past experiments and on the method of transmission.

"Why was the choice of destruction at the transmitting end made," Lydia inquired?

This really made her nervous. If she weren't already on the edge of death, she wasn't sure she would want to take the chance.

"The huge energy release and our ability to utilize this energy for transmission and reconstitution, makes this approach feasible. If we had to generate the energy required for transmission, we would dim the lights of San Antonio every time," Tom replied.

"Also, if we only obtained the atom-by-atom information and used a different source of energy for reconstitution we would end up with two copies of the same individual," Linda added.

"Finally, if you are going to open up space, the receiving end will likely have only a minimum of available energy. If we needed to establish a high energy source at the receiving end, space would need to be conquered before we got there. You can immediately understand the benefit of this approach," Aaron added.

"So, you got the pigs through. How much did each pig weigh," Darian asked?

"The pigs weighed in at two hundred and two hundred and fifty pounds," Aaron spoke up.

"We took detailed pictures of each one. I was familiar with every hair, every nick, and every spot on the pig's skin. We took full body MRI's and a full set of X-rays. These pigs are the most thoroughly examined animals anywhere in the world.

The only thing difference that I could find, between the transmitted pig and the reconstituted pig, seemed to be the elimination of some skin scar tissue. All of our successful transmissions have been under observation and they all seem to be the same animal that we thoroughly tracked and recorded prior to transmission," he continued.

"Well, I feel so much better knowing that a pig went first and survived. Did he talk the same when you interviewed him after the transmission," Joe said in a slow exaggerated drawl?

He felt better knowing that the transmitter was capable of successfully transmitting an animal larger than himself.

"I guess the pigs are safe from becoming bacon or sausage," Darian added.

"Yes, they will probably be pampered for the rest of their lives and outlive all of us. They will have monthly and then later yearly tests to check their condition for the rest of their natural lives," Aaron explained.

Well, the three of you are now in the know about our efforts. Tomorrow we will hold the first of what I expect to be three successful transmissions," Jorge said as he slowly pointed to each of the three transmission candidates.

"Lydia is first. She will be on a liquid only diet after eight this evening. This afternoon my wife is hosting us to a grilled steak dinner. The steak is compliments of Joe's father and his uncle. This is their second care package to me," Jorge announced.

"Please arrange the work so you arrive by five thirty. We want Lydia to have time to enjoy dinner before she begins her fast."

Jorge had moved the three into the officers' rows of homes on base to improve the security he felt was needed to protect them and the program.

The three were able to walk over to Jorge's home for the grilled steak dinner.

"I don't think I can eat," Lydia said later as they were getting ready to sit down in the gazebo in Jorge's back yard.

"Well, you take what you want. Try one bite of the steak. I am sure my Dad picked the best cow and Uncle Ted probably tried to outdo himself in getting the steak marinated. I will eat whatever you don't want," Joe said as he sat down next to her.

"Thanks, I appreciate that. How about you get your plate, and I will just take a bite of meat from your piece. The grilled vegetables look good so I will try a normal helping. However, how about letting me have just the end of your potato," Lydia replied.

"It's a deal," Joe said as stood and went for his food. He returned with an extra plate of grilled vegetables and an extra place setting.

Lydia and he seemed to have a natural feel for each other. This was the first time Joe felt relaxed around the opposite sex.

Darian, Lydia, and Joe left later together later in the evening. It was clear that the rest of the team would stay for several more hours.

The three walked back to their new living quarters.

"That was really a great feast," Darian said as he walked backwards ahead of the two for a moment to talk to them.

"Do you eat steaks like that at home," he continued?

"Yes, about once a week. Uncle Ted likes to mix the meats. He does pork, chicken, beef, goat, lamb on a consistent basis. Once a week or every other week he cooks vegetarian dishes. He is a real Chef by training, but he never wanted to work away from the ranch," Joe replied.

"Was he ever married," Lydia asked.

"Not that I know of," Joe replied.

He suspected that both his Dad and Ted had been in love with his mother.

"Well, they must have changed shifts. These are different guards around the house," Joe observed.

"How is everything," Joe inquired of the clean-cut seasoned sergeant.

"I need to learn the insignias of these guys" he thought to himself.

"Doing good, everything is in order," was the friendly but formal reply.

The guards were posted in front and back and one in the house itself. The one in the house was set up in the dining room that was more or less in the middle of the first floor.

There were three separate bedrooms upstairs. Each of them had their own bathroom and shower.

The fourth upstairs room was like a big family room. It was appointed with a large couch, two easy chairs, a large flat screen television and a wet bar. The bar was stocked, and the refrigerator held a mix of soft drinks and some beer.

Joe and Darian both ribbed Lydia about the fact that she had the biggest and best room.

"Well good night," they said to each other as they each went to their rooms.

Joe took a shower and then took his book to the family room. He loved to read but had not had the time while he was going to school. He figured he might as well feed his mind for as long as he could.

The easy chairs were especially comfortable, and he settled in with a tumbler of crushed ice and Pellegrino.

"I can't get to sleep. Will I bother you if I sit on the couch," Lydia asked as she came into the room carrying her comforter.

"It would be my pleasure," Joe replied.

"She looks great and smells delicious," he thought to himself.

He was not used to having someone to talk to and wasn't sure what to expect or what to do. At home not more than a few dozen words were wasted in idle conversation.

Usually, Uncle Ted would tell some variation of the stories he seemed to always have available.

"I am so nervous about tomorrow that sleep seems impossible. How can you stand to be the last?

If Jorge had not made me the first, I think I would have said no," Lydia said as she curled up on the end of the couch with the light blanket, she had brought with her.

"Well, I figure it's first to the dinner table and last to everything else," Joe said slowly with a grin.

This was an Uncle Ted saying though Joe had heard many variations of the same saying.

"Well, what if I don't make it," Lydia inquired.

She already felt better just talking with Joe.

"Well, that would be a sad state of affairs. To be out done by a pig that is," Joe said with a chuckle.

"It would be hell since I would really like to spend more time with you," he thought to himself.

A smile from Lydia was the reward Joe had been looking for.

"Yes, I guess you're right. I don't want to be outdone by a pig either.

I hear that the first pig was a male and that Linda named him Tom because of its reddish hue. Tom got back at her by declaring the female pig was named Linda. I have caught them teasing each other about it. They make such a great couple," Lydia replied.

"Yes, they have been married for thirty-five years and it's clear that they are really great friends as well as more or less collaborative genius inventors.

Joe was expecting a reply but realized that Lydia was dozing off. He turned down his reading light slightly and just watched her for a while.

Lydia stretched out and fell asleep. Her feet were sticking out of the end of the wrap or blanket she was in, so Joe quietly got up and covered her feet with the blanket that was folded up on the end of the couch. He turned off the light and took the seat in the other easy chair that faced the door and the couch.

He spent the next few minutes taking in Lydia's figure and then fell asleep.

The next day, the test was delayed because Jorge was called away to a critical call.

The Brazilian transmission project had run into a dead end and had contacted the US to see if they could get help. Jorge understood their frustration, but he was not going to give them any information about his team's effort.

"I appreciate your frustration. We have had similar ones as well. I would like to help but our current relationship prohibits the close cooperation that could be available," Jorge pointed out.

"Yes, perhaps we can help each other both technically and financially," Manfredo Silva replied.

He knew he had the financial depth that would be of interest to Jorge's team.

"Would it be possible to meet in person and discuss the options for a combined effort," Manfredo proposed.

He was thinking about the effort the Brazilian team had made. Their progress had run into a wall in the transmission of living matter. From plants and insects to the simplest cell, the results had all been failure.

"I would welcome some discussion on this topic. I understand you have already recruited some personnel for duty in the longer-term deployment of the results of this effort," Jorge replied.

He wanted Manfredo to know his team was watching but he was truly interested in the additional recruits.

"Yes, that is so but we may be ahead of ourselves," Manfredo replied.

"Let's meet in about three weeks. Meanwhile let's discuss how we can work together both in the short term and then in the long term," Jorge suggested.

Jorge was interested in access to the new Brazilian rocket launch sites as well as the volunteers that had been recruited.

Finally, the Brazilian effort was well financed. The money would become useful when the final building of the Door distribution fleet hit its peak.

"I look forward to the meeting. Where should we meet," Manfredo inquired?

"Let's meet at the Kennedy Space Center. This will provide the best location for our teams to get together," Jorge suggested.

He was not going to mention or bring anyone to his current project site. He anticipated both a Russian and Chinese fishing trawler would be cruising legally off the coast to monitor the meeting. He intended to feed them all the misleading information he could.

Manfredo left the meeting with the realization that he would be recommending Brazil to join the American led effort. He would have to tell a reluctant Brazilian government that their program was stalled and that their best bet would be to lend support to what he hoped would be a more successful US led effort.

He did not want to join any of the other efforts because the approach of these other efforts did not seem to be having more success but seemed to have a fatal flaw. They were achieving duplication but not transmission.

Jorge left the call and went to meet with his team.

"I just got of the line with Manfredo Silva the leader of the Brazilian transmission project. They have hit the wall in their efforts, and they don't have a wild scientist like Tom to make the winning mistakes," Jorge said as he smiled at Tom.

"Honest, I didn't do it on purpose," Tom lied with a brilliant smile showing.

"After all, doing the same thing over and over and expecting a different result is really the sign of being mad," he once again thought to himself.

"I have set up a meeting with Manfredo. I have set the date far enough into the future so we will know where our project stands.

Once we get through with our initial transmissions, we will want to move on to the transmission of healthy candidates.

The Brazilians have already recruited several volunteers. We have reviewed their status and they will fit right into our effort. And I have interviewed and received acceptances from several potential candidates here in the US.

And Tom and Linda have interviewed several in Europe.

The Brazilians also have a sizeable pot of money allocated to build space vessels. This should help us accelerate our program. Are there any questions," Jorge concluded?

"Yes, I have been following up on the recruits that have been identified by our various field recruiters. Should I go ahead and get them here," Jacque inquired?

"Please do so.

We will want to get all the recruits here at the same time so they can begin to train together. We will also want to see if we have compatible people that can travel together for the extended time they will be in space," Jorge continued.

"Phil you will want to process all the recruits through our top-secret security clearance process," Jorge said as he looked over to the only other military member of the team.

"Yes, I believe all the candidates are on our list and being processed. So far there seems to be no problem," Phil replied.

"Again, let's target their arrival to the time just after we have our third successful transmission," Jorge reiterated.

"We have recruits from the US, England, and Germany. They are all awaiting a reply from us. Until now we didn't feel it appropriate to get them fully into the program. Each recruit has had an initial screening and has been cleared. We are processing each candidate for a top-secret security clearance. Once they get cleared, we will be ready to send out our acceptance letters," Ryan spoke up.

Ryan had been working with Phil and had been ready for weeks. He had been waiting for the success of the transmissions. The next three weeks would be the final hurdle. Then they would all look to him and wonder why they were not farther along on getting on to the next phase.

He knew the drill.

Suddenly the project manager would not be doing a good enough job.

Chapter 8: Transmission

Butterflies are common in the moments leading up to some big event. Ball players visualize their shot or their pitch. Speakers go through their speech another time before going up to the podium.

Lydia faced a different problem. She could not imagine; she could not rehearse. There was no previous experience to calibrate what would happen. She chose to think about the time she had sat and enjoyed the sunrise as she sat on the hill not far from her house.

Tom was more nervous. He had killed almost a thousand mice during the development of the transmission capability. Mouse number one thousand had been a participant in every transmission since. It still seemed to be the same mouse. But how would he know?

Now it would be a human. Even though Lydia faced a death more terrible than a transmission failure, Tom did not want her death on his head.

He had butterflies as he worried for Lydia.

This was a nerve-racking and ultimate concern for Tom.

Every member was waiting in concerned anticipation at the receive end.

The only two people missing were Joe and Darian. They were the next two to be transmitted. They would not be allowed to witness this first transmission.

Lydia paced nervously and pulled the robe tightly around her as she waited for Tom to get everything ready for transmission.

She was thinking about last night and how comfortable it had been to be with Joe. He was shy and a true gentleman but also, he seemed to know how to defuse her tense situation. She was happy to have this memory as she contemplated the transmission.

She really did not expect to live and the warm memory from the previous night was a treasure for her.

"I will be at the receiving end waiting for you. Should I bring you the robe at the chamber door or do you prefer for me to wait outside," Joe teased her as they came out to the van that had come to pick her up?

"I only have orders to pick a Lydia up," the young airman said when Joe asked for the ride.

"Well, you are doing that. I just need a ride over to building 51. I think you are taking her to building 37. Am I right? You can drop me on the way," Joe said as he got into the front seat of the van.

He had no plans to get back out of the van.

"I guess that would be OK," was the reply. Building 51 was on the way.

The transmitter was always first tested with "the" mouse. This took the minimal power but verified everything was working.

"I have the mouse," was the signal that all had gone well.

The mouse was also Tom's continuing testing of the stability of the system and the process. Today he was using the "same" mouse that had been sent on the first successful transmission. This would be the mouse's 100th transmission. There seemed to be no change in the mouse. It always seemed to be the same mouse and seemed to retain the memory it had of all the mazes it was tested in.

This ability to reconstitute and have the memory intact was one of the most important and amazing aspects of the reconstitution. Tom had worried the most about the mental reconstitution. How was he to know that it was happening the way he wanted it to?

Now he was about to try it on an actual person, and it mattered a lot to him. He had voiced his doubts to Linda on the prior evening.

"Tom, we have tested this process to the fullest. I am worried too, but this is the right next step. I will buy you a cold one to drink with me at the end of the bar when we succeed tomorrow," had been Linda's reply before kissing Tom on the forehead.

"Relax, I know you are nervous, but Linda will greet you. I will not let anything happen to you," Tom said to Lydia with more confidence than he was actually feeling.

He was as nervous as Lydia. That Lydia came out the other end as the same Lydia was the single most important test he would face.

This time it would be on a real person.

"I do so want that cold beer," Tom mumbled to himself.

"They told me you were here and asking to be let in," Linda said she greeted Joe.

"You are welcome in the lab until the actual moment of transmission. At that point only I and my assistant will be in the room. We will bring Lydia out to the examination room across the hallway. You're welcome to wait in the hallway during transmission.

You can greet her but then she will be run through all the tests you have experienced yourself. At that point you may as well go about what you want to do until we meet as a team in the late afternoon," Linda had informed him.

"Young romance, not good in this situation," she thought to herself.

"Let me help you get into position," Jacqueline said as she took Lydia's hand and guided her into the chamber. Jacqueline was normally not involved in the transmission process.

Her participation had been sought out only because of Lydia's gender.

"Now relax, think of something pleasant and hold still. I will take your robe. Don't worry, I will keep Tom from gawking. If he takes too long in hitting the switch, I will slap him on the back of his head," Jacqueline joked as she positioned Lydia and then backed out of the chamber.

She hoped she was not transmitting her personal anxiety to Lydia.

Tom was ready. As soon as the door was closed and Jacqueline pushed the seal switch, Tom pushed the transmit switch.

The flash always caught him by surprise and this time he let out a small grunt.

"Is everything OK," Jacqueline asked as she came around to the control center?

Just then they both heard Linda's excited transmission.

"I have the mouse, Oh, thank God, I have the mouse. And she is a beauty. Yes, Yes, Yes."

Tom let out his breath. He had not realized he was holding it.

"Yes! She has the mouse," He yelled and took Jacqueline's hand and danced a quick hopping jig.

This had been the most stressful transmission to date that he had conducted.

Tom was done for the day. It was only eight am and he was ready for his beer. He left the lab to got to see the results of Lydia's examination.

The medical personnel were at the receiving end, and they immediately took over and transported Lydia to the special hospital wing that had been prepared for this occasion.

"Congrats on making it through. You have made it easier for the rest of us," Joe said in greeting as Lydia gave him a hug in the hallway.

"Thanks for being here and thanks for last night," she had whispered in his ear during their brief hug.

"I am not allowed to go in with you, but I will be keeping a close eye on what goes on," Joe called in as the door was closed on him.

Lydia felt a surge of warmth.

She had at least two dozen wires attached to her body. Her brain was being scanned. Her internal organs were being monitored and she would soon be wheeled away to get a total body CAT scan.

She was to be put into observation around the clock for the next three days. Even a bone marrow sample would be drawn. The last time that had been the most painful of all the tests.

There was a special food menu for her as well. She could order anything she wanted any time of the day as long as it was on the menu. To her surprise the menu was quite extensive.

She was a little amazed at her surroundings. The room had a small couch that could be made into a sleeper. There was a leather recliner, an area rug and coffee table, a desk area and a large flat screen television and a single automated articulating bed.

She was free to walk around, sit on the couch or lay in the bed.

After the initial surge of nurses, aids, and a variety of doctors all bent on getting her situated, wired up and interrogated, she was allowed to do as she pleased as long as she stayed in her room

They had posted two armed guards at the door.

Lydia had by this time been mentally checked out by Jacqueline. However, she would be getting additional interviews and tests to determine if she was still the Lydia that had stepped into the transmitter end.

"Well, your responses all match the answers you gave before the transmission. And you certainly look exactly like the person that went into the transmission chamber," Jacqueline had shared with her.

"I think I have become a Christmas tree," she joked with Aaron when he came into chat with her. She had wires attached to her head, her chest and back, even her ankles, thighs, and mid-section.

All of these wires came to a small transmitting unit attached by a belt to her waist. The data was constantly being transmitted to a computer that was comparing every aspect of her being to the data they had collected in a similar manner before the transmission.

"What is your name and date of birth," Aaron asked?

"Lydia Jade Tabata, June 16, 2014," was her response. That was the first question every individual asked before proceeding to talk to her.

"How old are you," Aaron asked next?

"Why chronologically, I am twenty-two. Mentally, after this ordeal I am an old maid of eighty," Lydia joked with Aaron.

"How do you feel," Aaron continued?

"Actually refreshed, something like coming out of a nice cold shower on a hot day," Lydia said as she looked around and was struck by the grand view from her window.

"Did I actually get reconstituted?" she asked.

"Yes, you did. Who am I," Aaron continued his simple questioning?

"You are Aaron Alton. Known to your team as the thinker," Lydia replied as she looked away from the nurse taking a series of blood samples for testing.

With all the advanced sensing techniques, the blood work was still required.

Late the next day the team was getting its first full results report.

"Let's begin with the most startling outcome of our transmission," Jorge said as he looked around the table.

He had been briefed the day before. He had reported the findings all the way to the President.

He had asked Joe and Darian not to attend the current meeting.

"Why are we not allowed at the meeting," Darian had asked worriedly?

"Because something is radically different than was expected," Joe replied.

"Did she make it," Darin asked nervously? He was next and he did not want to come out drooling or in some vegetative state. Dead was OK, but misery was not.

"She made it fine, and she was Lydia as far as I could tell," Joe said as he realized Lydia had given him a positive message by mentioning the previous night.

"Dr. Leslie Marigold, breast cancer specialist is here to give her report," Jorge said quietly.

"Lydia's breast cancer has been totally eliminated. There is not a single trace of it in her body. I have repeated the tests three times. And she has had as many, full body, CAT scans. I don't know what to say other than it's a miracle," Dr. Marigold stated succinctly.

"This is an outcome none of us expected but it certainly will have a dramatic impact on the world. Think of the impact it will have," Tom reiterated his thoughts in rapid fire as he looked around the room.

He had suspected as much from the performance of the animals he had transmitted. His little mouse seemed to always be in better shape.

"Has Lydia been told," Jacqueline inquired?

"No, we have not shared the results with anyone other than with the General and now this team," Dr. Marigold replied.

"However, she knows something is up. She keeps asking about the results as if she knows something truly unusual has happened."

Lydia knew that she felt very different than before the transmission. She felt really energetic like her old self. She had tried to extract the findings of all the tests, but the doctors and nurses were being evasive. She had taken three CT scans and knew something unexpected had taken place.

She was not as experienced as Jacqueline, but she didn't need to be, to see something unusual had happened and the people around her were being evasive.

"I think I am cancer free," the thought unexpectedly came to her and at that instant she knew she was right.

She could feel it. It was as if the weight of the world had lifted.

"Let's bring her here and give her the official news," Jorge said and turned to one if his aids and quietly gave her the instructions to bring Lydia to the meeting.

"We will not share this with our other two volunteers. I do not want to give them false hope. If this is a consistent outcome there will be a totally new and separate effort launched by a medical team. It will be a separate effort that we will coach but we will keep the Door program on track.

That is an order from the President," Jorge said looking around at his team.

Though this was monumental in its impact on the world, his orders were to keep the Door project on a fast track. His team was not to be distracted. These orders had come from the President. She was adamant that nothing was to get in the way.

She insisted they get the Door program into space by the end of the year. She recognized that a successful Door program would translate to her success.

After the outcome on the previous day Tom was pouring over his analysis.

"Linda, I have gone over the theoretical equations of dissolution and reconstitution. It is driving me crazy that I missed the fact that the reconstitution process does not create deviant growths," Tom said as he looked up from his desk to where Linda sat across from him at her desk.

They shared a large home office. Their desks faced each other. They had come to this arrangement when they realized they often spent endless hours, reading, studying, and theorizing at their desks. Their current office was in their home in the officer's quarters. It was one of the humbler homes in a pristine neighborhood. They had selected the house they were in because of this one room that comfortably accommodated their desk arrangement.

"Why would you be surprised? You had the polarity of the whole process out by 180 degrees.

Admit it, it was only your intuition that made you change the dissolution polarity on the 1000th mouse," Linda smiled as she delivered her reply.

"Well, I had already killed the other nine hundred ninety-nine. What difference would one more make," Tom said in his defense.

"Crazy was killing nine hundred, ninety-nine mice because you expected some different outcome by doing the same thing over and over and over," Linda said as she gave Tom a kiss on the forehead.

This she knew always went through his mind.

"However all that aside I would really like your help to better understand these reconstitution equations and theorems.

Also, I noticed that one of our recruits has actually been pursuing a master's degree on this topic. I am curious what his professors have been teaching him and what they may know," Tom continued.

The written profile of Harold Hatfield Hastly also referred to as H cubed, one of the Door recruits had caught Tom's eye. The young man was from the Oregon Coast and was getting his current education from Dartmouth.

Jorge had personally gone and recruited him to come into the program. Tom hoped he was as smart as his major professor had alluded.

"It is likely to lead these recruits to being the virtual prisoners of this program," Linda said as she motioned around the room with her hands.

She was absolutely sure every word they spoke was being recorded. It was also likely they were being visually recorded as well.

It made being romantic very difficult. However, she loved to tease Tom and she was not about to stop because of potential voyeurs. She loved to see his face turn red as he melted at her advances.

He too suspected they were being watched.

Jorge stopped the meeting and addressed Tom.

"Tom are you with us," Jorge inquired as he realized his brilliant scientist was daydreaming.

"I am sorry if these details are boring you," Jorge said in a joking tone.

"My apology, I was going over a discussion Linda and I had about the equations of reconstitution," Tom replied.

"Mostly true," he thought to himself.

He knew his face was red and Linda was sitting across from him with her Cheshire smile. She knew what he had been thinking about.

"Welcome Lydia we are all pleased with your successful transmission and reconstitution. We will now go over our learning and the first successful outcome," Jorge continued.

"I knew it. I knew it," was Lydia's excited response when Dr. Marigold shared the fact that no cancer cells could be detected.

Lydia stood up and came around the table and gave Tom a hug and kiss on his forehead.

"Thank you," she said as once again Tom's face turned red.

Then she proceeded to go around the room and hug everyone and thank them.

"Thank you for letting me go first," Lydia said as she finished by giving Jorge a hug.

"We are all ecstatic about this result. However, we will not tell the other two volunteers. I do not want to plant false hope. I hope their outcome is the same as yours," Jorge continued.

"Because of Lydia's results, I have been asked from the very top of the chain of command to accelerate the next two transmissions.

The next transmission is to be the day after tomorrow. It will be followed three days later with the final transmission," Jorge continued.

"This will put us almost a month ahead of our critical path schedule," Ryan said as he projected the critical path schedule on the large flat screen.

"Will you be pulling forward the other activities with the recruits and your meetings with the Brazilians?"

"Let's get the next two transmissions completed and then we will adjust all activities associated with getting the Doors out to space," Jorge replied.

"Yes, indeed," he thought, "the pressure was mounting to go faster."

Lydia was listening to the discussion in the room but all she could think of was that she had a new lease on life.

She was now also thinking of Joe.

He had been sitting reading a magazine out in the hallway when she was escorted out to come to this meeting.

"Well, transmission and reconstitution seems to become you," he had drawled as he walked next to the attendant wheeling her to the pickup area.

"What are you doing sitting out here," she had asked?

She had been somewhat surprised.

"Well, hospitals always bothered me.

I wanted to make sure they didn't take you to the dissection room," Joe had joked.

Two days later, Darian was pacing nervously. He knew Lydia had made it through. He had not seen her, but word was her transmission had happened without any problems.

He had been spending the days getting some sun at the officer's pool and flirting with the young female officers.

Now it was his turn. He should have talked to Lydia to see how she felt. Somehow, he always got distracted by the opposite sex.

"Not to worry," Tom said as he gave Darian a pat on his shoulder.

"I will make sure you get there as safe as this mouse," he continued as he put the mouse in the middle of the chamber.

Darian watched the mouse through the observation chamber port hole. There was a bright flash and the mouse disappeared.

"How big of a flash will I make," he asked as he turned to look at Tom in an alarmed manner?

"I have the mouse, I have the mouse," came out of the speakers on the wall.

"Oh, a thousand times brighter," Tom replied as he guided a shaking Darian into position and helped him remove his robe.

"Well, no wonder the ladies like him," Tom thought as he closed the chamber.

He walked to the control consul, looked in to see that Darian was still in place and pressed the transmit button.

Three days later Joe went through the same process. He was much calmer than Lydia and Darian. He had anticipated some sort of failure, but he was now aware that something unusual but positive was happening. The fact that the schedule had been advanced was an indication that success was being achieved and the desire to go faster had surfaced.

He knew Lydia was feeling upbeat about something. They had not been allowed to talk to each other, but she smiled and waved each time they saw each other.

This time as Joe was taken to his hospital room, it was Lydia that greeted him. She ran up to his wheelchair, gave him a hug and a kiss on the cheek before he was wheeled into his room.

He put his hand on his cheek. He could feel his face turn red. He could feel his heart race.

A few days later Joe, Darian and Lydia were all sitting in the same meeting room with the rest of the Door team.

"Success, Success, Success, we are all here to celebrate success," Jorge said pointing slowly at each one of them as he bent slightly toward them.

"I am so happy about what this means to the three of you. Your cancers are cured," Jorge continued as he shook each of their hands and gave them each a hug.

"You're a General and you are acting like their father," he caught himself thinking as he tried not to tear up.

It would be unbecoming for a General to cry in front of his team.

He stopped for a moment, and no one missed the heartfelt mood he was in at the moment.

"I have talked to each of you separately and each of you has agreed to be part of the Door program. Thank you. I am so proud to have you on the team," he said as he looked around the room.

Tom gave out a hurrah and everyone began to clap.

"Now let's get to the business at hand. Ryan, please share the new Door activation critical path schedule we have developed in the last few days," Jorge said after the clapping stopped.

The news of the transmission successes and the ability to cure cancer had created a totally new and unplanned situation.

He was being pressured to accelerate the Door program and to manage the transfer of the transmission technology to fifty hospitals, one in each state.

He then announced, "We are all going to take time for a breather. Tom and Linda are returning to their home in England where their daughter is about to give birth. Each of us will take time off until after the Fourth of July.

Then we will come back, and all Hell will be turned loose. Each of us will be going full blast.

All the recruits will be assembled and go through a crash course. Jacqueline and Aaron will be evaluating and training them.

I have asked Joe, Darian, and Lydia to be part of the training team. They are veterans of the transmission process. The three of them and all the recruits will go through the same program as our astronauts have in the past. However, they will do this at a very accelerated pace and abbreviated time frame.

The recruits will be matched for compatibility. They will go out into space in teams of six. They will be out for a very long time. For them it will seem to be a few years, for us back on Earth it may be our lifetimes.

I will meet with the Brazilians tomorrow. If all goes as I believe it will, they will have their recruits here at the same time as those we have recruited.

Any questions," Jorge finished one of his longest speeches to the team?

"We are getting the people ready, how is the production of the "Spaceships" and the "Doors" coming," Aaron asked?

He was not sure what they were calling the vessels that would carry the doors.

"I will be reviewing that progress and will report back to this team after the Fourth," Jorge replied.

He had made the same point to Madam President when she pushed him to go faster.

"General, find out and tell them they have to the end of the year to put all the hardware into space," the President had replied.

It was clear to Jorge that every aspect of the effort would be pushed to its limit.

After a brief set of questions, the meeting ended, and the team spent some time just chatting before departing.

Chapter 9: The President

Technological breakthrough often disrupts the forward change and improvement vectors of a culture or country.

The ability to sail long distances by the Europeans empowered them to conquer much of the known world.

The ability to mass produce goods and run production assembly lines pushed the US into a position of world dominance as the twentieth century began.

The first satellite by the Russians surprised the world and energized the US to a new level of technical competition.

The establishment of the internet and then the I-phone empowered some of the most subjugated peoples of the world. It changed the entire cultural fabric of the entire world and was continuing to do so.

A breakthrough in healthcare that changed all fundamental approaches was potentially derailing for every country in the world. It would affect all economies.

President Lacy MacAdam sat contemplating these facts as she reviewed the report on her desk.

She had called her cabinet members in for a conference session to discuss the new twist that their administration was experiencing.

The first three humans to have been transmitted were chosen because they were young, and they each had terminal cancer and had only six months or so to live. Cancer free after transmission and healthier than most everyone else, they represented a new era of medical treatment.

The elimination of the cancers was an unexpected side effect of the Door program that had surprised everyone who was involved.

The discovery of a new technology that in fact eradicated all cancers and other diseases from the body would radically alter the condition and lives of almost all the people in the world.

Stanley Black, science advisor to the President, had been sent out to learn how this technology worked and to report back to the cabinet.

"Madam President, I met with Tom and Linda Hughes and watched the transmission of a mouse to see how the system worked. I have never experienced anything like I did at the test lab.

It is fascinating and counter intuitive. I don't understand the mathematics and the physical manipulation of dissolution and reconstitution.

Tom and Linda are the brains behind it all. They both laughed when I asked how they had made the breakthrough.

They went on about reversing polarity and threw out some additional theoretical jargon.

Then they both looked at each other and once again laughed, "pure luck" they both said in unison.

I told them we all should all be so lucky.

I will say that I think that General Jorge Martinez has followed a sound path in guiding the development, testing of the transmission process and how he recruited the human subjects. The team worked up from a mouse to the successful transmission of three human subjects. There are mice, rats, rabbits, goats, sheep, and a few pigs transmitted successfully before a human subject was considered. All animals were successful participants in the transmission process. They are all being monitored, and all seem to be in excellent health.

Our intelligence reports that all the other competing efforts have been able to transmit and reconstitute non-living matter but have made no progress with living matter.

Brazil has officially asked to become part of our program," Stan stated near the end of his presentation.

"We need to come up with a policy to manage this situation and to quickly spread this capability across the country.

We also need to keep most what we know secret as long as possible.

If we don't act quickly, we are likely to have riots demanding that we make this available to everyone.

I don't want to politicize this situation but how we handle this could be of huge benefit to our efforts to make health care less costly.

The question will be how many other diseases does this process cure?

It appears to reconstitute the body in its healthiest form. I have a hunch it will cause a dramatic change in the health care industry. Their stock values will plunge if this is handled wrong.

I want this team to discuss the impact of a society that can cure all ills. It will cause an economic upheaval larger than any we have ever experienced before," Lacy addressed her still silent cabinet members.

"I think it is even more dramatic than just the reaction of the people in our country.

Think of the implication for all the governments in the world. Each will be destabilized by a population that knows that we have a technology that cures all ills, and their country does not," Secretary of State Craig Lebak commented.

"This will create worldwide chaos," he continued.

"I agree with you Craig. We will need to have an outreach effort with all the countries in the world. Craig, I am putting you in charge of determining what that entails. We will need to move slowly when making the total capability known.

We need to manage this transition very carefully and in a controlled manner.

Meanwhile we need to prepare our country and ourselves.

Let's figure out the approach to managing this situation," President MacAdam concluded.

"One of the first things I suggest is to increase the security around this technology and the people working on it," Craig voiced his concern.

He was immediately concerned about direct sabotage or even physical attack on the people or the technology.

"Additionally, we should convene a meeting of all the key leaders around the world. We will need to converge on a global approach if we want to have any hope of managing this without worldwide chaos," Craig continued.

"Dam her luck," Mathew Pinkerton III thought to himself.

Everything she touches turns to gold.

He was in the same party as her and had lost out to her early in the presidential primaries. He had a great dislike for her but had taken the role as Secretary of Defense so he could stay in the spotlight, the Presidential game and in a position where he could intervene when he thought necessary.

"I agree with Craig. We need to make sure this effort is kept out of the public eye," Mathew said in support.

But in fact, how to disrupt the program was what was whirling through his mind.

"I will have to see how I can turn this gold into lead," Mathew thought as the meeting broke up and he left for his office.

"Thank you, Mathew for your support," a surprised Lacy said to him.

Mathew was consistently the neigh sayer. She had recognized early on in the primary campaign that he had strong financial backing and was potentially a long-term liability. She had asked him to be on her cabinet as she followed the old saying *"keep your friends close and you enemies even closer."*

She had invited him to become part of her cabinet so she could influence the section of the party that supported him.

Craig, on the other hand, had been recruited because of his natural talent in dealing with a wide variety of people. He always quickly analyzed the situation around him and came up with rational and actionable steps to take. He was her go to person on almost all issues.

"I will contact the General and get security beefed up. I will take your advice and convene a global meeting to address this breakthrough. Let's discuss the timing of such a meeting. I am inclined to wait for two things.

First, I want our Door mission to be on its way and second, I want the production facilities of the transmit-receive units to be in place," Lacy continued.

"Craig, I would like you to organize and coordinate this activity," Lacy said looking at him.

"I will get my team on it immediately," Craig replied.

Chapter 10: Door Ships

The roar and the fiery exhaust of rockets firing off into Space, astronauts in shielded helmets going hand over hand across the surface of the spaceship, the rotation of the ship in the movie 2001 and the single awake astronaut. These are the pictures that come to mind when people think about being out in space.

They also think of the action and adventure portrayed by beautiful actresses and actors.

Most real astronauts would snicker and laugh at that image.

If it were not for the experiments and the scientific studies the time in space would be miserable. It is also devastating to the human condition. Humans are gravity conditioned animals. The lack of gravity has many adverse effects on the human body.

General Jerald Delaney, US Marine Core was in charge of getting the Door transport ships into space.

His team had started their ship building efforts several years before in anticipation of the solar system space race. The ship's specifications had been altered when the concept of the Door technology began to take shape.

The design had always been in the shape of a donut. It would rotate and produce a one G field against the outer diameter floor. However, the name spaceship continued to be used.

"Space donuts for the name would require, space cops and donut shops." Jerry thought as he smiled to himself.

Now the spokes in the center would be built to accommodate the Door modules.

He was glad he had been pressing his team to get their ships ready to be assembled in space.

The initial specifications called for an unbelievable level of radiation shielding. So much shielding that the team had been stumped.

"We don't have enough g... d... lift capacity to achieve the desired shielding," one of his top design engineers had said in frustration as she threw down her pen.

"And she is the most religious of the team," Jerry thought as he listened to the team agree with her.

"We have separated the construction of our space wheels from getting them properly shielded. Let's create a small but heavily shielded living area and leave the rest of the structure lightly shielded. One of you will have a brilliant shielding idea once we get it all assembled," Jerry had coached his team.

"Aye, Aye sir," his team had replied in unison.

The one ex-marine on the team just gave an unenthusiastic, "Huu...ra," as the team went back to work.

They all knew when Jerry was ready to move on.

General Jorge Martinez, his long-time friend in the Air Force was the one who solved the problem by reminding him that other than an astronomical energy needed, most of the shielding could be put in place with the matter transmission technology.

"I didn't come over to kibitz," Jorge said after pointing out what he took as obvious.

"I came to synchronize our efforts. Madam President has put me in charge of getting our Doors technology into space. Your spaceships will be designated and put into use as Door transports," Jorge explained.

"Well, what does this mean to me," Jerry asked.

"How about we go to the officers club and discuss this over a cold one."

Later at the club they sat in a private room discussing the Door program.

"The spaceships will each need to carry nine Doors. Each will deploy eight doors. One Door will be part of the spaceship itself," Jorge shared.

"What do these Doors do," Jerry asked in curiosity.

"They will allow the transmission of a person to the destination of the Door," Jorge had shared.

This discussion had taken place last year shortly after the successful transmission of the mouse.

The President had immediately put the pressure on both the spaceship building effort and the Door project.

Now almost a year later, Jorge once again put in a call again to Jerry.

"So, you want to talk to me again. I suppose you want me to go even faster," Jerry had responded when Jorge called him up.

"Shall we meet at the officer's quarters," Jorge countered?

This time they had dinner. Jorge ordered a rare prime rib and a Margarita.

"I was called in this morning and ended up getting orders from the Lady herself. I am to get my space vessels up by the end of the year. I hope I don't provide the Fourth of July's fireworks in January," Jerry commented as he took a bite of his steak.

"Yes, and I have been ordered to have my doormen and the Doors ready to go at that same time.

"How has your team decided to carry the Doors," Jorge inquired?

"They will become the cross spokes of the wheel," Jerry replied.

He took out a piece of paper and scratched out a rough design.

"I can show you the drawings once we get back to my team's work area," he said after taking a drink of his ale.

"What about the radiation shielding," Jorge asked next?

"We have that mostly solved but the amount needed is still massive," Jerry said frowned and shook his head.

"What's changed to cause this massive push for speed," Jerry asked?

He was not expecting an answer from Jorge and was surprised when the answer was given.

"Honest, you have transmitted and recombined a human being," Jerry said quietly?

The magnitude of the achievement was unbelievable. Jerry had not expected such success to occur in his lifetime.

"Yes, we have been successful.

Another factor is that China has shown the willingness to risk its human volunteers. But As far as we know they have been having some problems with their reconstitution process," Jorge continued.

He did not share the other health improvement success that had been experienced by his team.

"Intelligence also has it that China is about at the same place as the US in getting some sort of space vessel built.

These two factors may give the US and its partners leverage in negotiating a deal where Earth sends out only one set of Doors and we all share them," Jorge replied.

He was not sharing the fact that the sharing would be within the solar system only.

Some of the doors were scheduled to go out beyond the solar system.

"I am meeting with the Brazilians in the next couple of days. They will be joining our efforts," Jorge shared.

"That means this half of the world and Europe is working together. That's encouraging," Jerry replied.

"To make this timing, I will need your team to assemble the structure we launch into space," Jerry said looking at Jorge.

"How much assembly are you talking about," Jorge asked?

"Actually, all of it," Jerry replied with a chuckle.

"What are we talking about," Jorge inquired as he thought about the young, inexperienced team he was assembling.

"Let's go back to the office and I will show you the drawings and the assembly concepts the team has developed.

They have come up with what they call a plug and play assembly approach. They have utilized every quick connect type of widget to make the assembly easy but solid and permanent," Jerry shared.

"Well, this certainly will provide my team with a challenge," Jorge said as the enormity of the effort to train his team of volunteers became clear.

"I will send part of my team over to learn how the assembly needs to occur. They will be tasked with coming up with ways to practice the assembly here on the ground," Jorge said as he traced his finger over the drawing on table in front of him.

"I hope Lydia, Joe and Darian can work some magic into this effort," Jorge was thinking as he continued to listen to Jerry.

"How about you show me this transmission reconstitution receiver set. And could I meet the first successful humans to be transmitted," Jerry asked?

The three people who were successfully transmitted will be on the team that I will send over to understand how to assemble the Doorships," Jorge offered.

"Well, I like the name *"Doorships."* I think you have just named the space vessels that we will send out," Jerry said as he repeated the name.

All stops had been pulled out by the West to make the journey to open up the solar system a United Nation's sponsored activity.

President Lacy McAdam had personally gone to the United Nations to present the amendment making the venture into the solar system an Earth alliance. She had used the analogy of the South Pole as a global effort to connect everyone to the fact that the world could work together when it chose to do so.

She was now going back once again to announce that the current Western Alliance had made a significant breakthrough and was targeting the coming year to begin its journey.

"I hope our intelligence is right about the stalled condition of the other programs. We believe that China has been able to reconstitute but the reconstitution is not one hundred percent. They replicate and don't know how to actually transmit. Their process needs a huge energy resource at the receiving end. This will make it almost impossible to use it in opening up the solar system," Lacy explained to her cabinet.

"I have called the leader of each country and made the same equal share proposal that we used in the past with the space station.

The Russians were the first to agree.

I believe the Chinese are ready to make it a joint venture.

India seems to be the most contentious," she continued.

"Larry, you're the ambassador to UN from the US. I want you to make the formal proposal and bring it to a vote," Lacy said as she pointed her finger at him to emphasize her point.

"I will put together the proposal. Once we get it agreement on this team, I will be pleased to take it to the council. This will take a minimum of a week.

Let's ensure that all the Security Council members agree to support it," Larry suggested.

Lacy went back to her office to attend to the other activities of being the President that she was required to keep moving forward.

Chapter 11: The Cleaning Job

The back window was opened in less than ten seconds. The side door opened effortlessly as the lock was picked. The break in proof car was hijacked in less than five seconds as its owner walked away from it. Professionals thieves are skilled, swift. And security is a Swiss Cheese word. Almost meaningless when the challenge is taken on by those truly interested in getting to what is supposed to be secure.

The Door program had the best security the country could afford. The rats in the system found the holes in the cheese. As usual the barn door was open, and no one recognized this fact.

The failure to see the open door was the reason Alice made the haul of a lifetime.

Alice's House Cleaning and Maid Service was prominently displayed on the six cleaning trucks owned by her company. She ran a legitimate and successful business. It paid for itself, and Alice received a good salary.

It was her side, off the record business that fueled her financial business bonus. This was a business she ran out of her head. There was nothing on paper. It was a business that she felt was almost legitimate. It certainly did not compare to or rake in the money that drug smuggling did, and it was happening all around her. The drug business made her scheme almost invisible.

Alice went into the smuggling business by accident. She had put some items in her cleaning truck and realized after she had re-entered the U.S. from a cleaning job in Mexico that the border guards never took notice of the goods.

The next time she went across she put some blue jeans and shoes in the truck and took them into Mexico. The search focused mostly on the drug trade. The search going into Mexico was cursory. The scrutiny on the trip back into the US was more thorough but focused on drugs.

Her cleaning vans were regular crossers and soon she had a working relationship with the border guards. Often in the morning she would bring them coffee. Since she never had any drugs in her vans, the sniffer dogs were never attracted to her vans and the inspectors soon became lax at checking for other items.

She made her money taking things into Mexico versus smuggling things into the US. This was counter to the action that got the attention of the inspectors.

She modified her cleaning vans by installing a raised floor. This provided a better way to conceal the goods being taken across the border.

She had personally done the modification work. This was the only way she knew how to keep what she was doing a secret. Once the floor was raised, she then put all her equipment racks back in. The modification was hard to notice.

She had designed foam inserts that were put in on her way going north so if the space were discovered and checked, she could claim it was a means of reducing the travel noise. This indeed happened and there were no questions asked.

She was very successful in taking stuff into Mexico. This success was the extra paycheck that she gave herself.

Though she refused to bring people across the border, her Mexican connections got in touch with her and got her into transporting individuals that had made it across the border.

Alice would arrange to deliver them to the desired US location. Sometimes she simply put them on a bus. Other times she would have someone drive them to the desired destination. Several times she got them a plane ticket.

She handled each situation based on where the individual was going and how much they were able to pay. Her fee was a simple one thousand dollars per adult. She did not charge for children if they were accompanied by an adult.

The unaccompanied children were the ones she would assign to a driver to deliver to a specific location.

This was another significant addition to her retirement account.

"I am just making sure I am not a burden on society and have my retirement taken care of," she rationalized her actions to herself.

When she was contacted about a special job that would pay in the millions, she curiously looked into it. She had been contacted because her company had entry passes to the Lakland air base to allow her cleaning trucks access to the various offices and homes her company serviced.

"Three million is not enough. It will take nine million for me to think about it," was her rebuff of the offer.

Alice figured her reply would end the conversation.

Her contact checked out her counteroffer. She was surprised when he replied that it had been accepted.

She had to reassess her position.

She requested the details to the specifics of what she was to do, and she wanted assurances that no one would get hurt.

"All you have to do is to park your cleaning van in the designated parking lot.

You will also rent an unmarked white truck and park it next to the cleaning van. Make sure you use cash to rent the white truck.

Leave the keys to both trucks under a brick in front of each truck. You will then pick up your cleaning truck and return it to your fleet at a specified time the next morning.

Additionally, you will map out the order that the cleaning gets done at each of the homes you clean. You will also provide the exact work that gets done and how to do it for in each home.

There is one address that we want specific information about. You will map the layout of this home and where the security cameras are located and how many guards and their location.

The third and final piece of information is a copy of your entry badges. Send a copy of a badge for a man and a badge for a woman. Fax these three items to the number that will be delivered to you by a messenger," she was told by her contact.

"And this is worth nine million dollars," was the question that went through her head but went unasked.

"That's it," Alice asked?

"Yes, and if you are asked you know nothing," came the reply.

"I really will know nothing she thought. I don't even know the guy on the phone," she thought to herself.

"Ok, sent half the money to the account that I will text you. Once that happens, I will do what you have asked," Alice instructed.

"This is serious business and on a grand scale. I will want to be gone as soon as possible after the first money transfer," Alice thought to herself. She figured if she never got the second half she would still have millions of dollars to live off of.

She planned to leave the country and go to Australia or maybe New Zealand.

She quickly arranged her finances.

This included establishing an offshore bank account. She asked around quietly to a variety of folks before she learned how to do this. Then she had to decide which offshore location would be the best for her.

She decided that more than one account would be the way to set it up. The four and a half million was in one account. Her personal savings was in a second account. She set up a third offshore account for the final four and a half million.

On a throw away phone she sent the account number to her contact. She then got rid of that phone by crushing it and dropping it into a random dumpster on one of her trips.

She processed the paperwork to give her nephew the cleaning business. She had her lawyer draw up the appropriate paperwork and then had her nephew attend a meeting where she formally turned the business over to him.

"This is a reward for the many years of good work you have put in helping me run the business," Alice had truthfully said as she transferred ownership to him.

The official transfer date would be the day after the truck was used. If the truck was traced back, he would be in the clear.

They would be after her. She had no illusions. She figured someone would trace the truck.

She made plane reservations from Beaumont, Texas to Seattle. On a separate arrangement she made a reservation from Seattle to Manila, from there to Singapore and then finally to Bangkok.

Her arrangements had a return leg. She knew a one-way ticket would raise a flag.

She would decide on her final destination once she had left the US.

For the next several weeks Alice accompanied the cleaners assigned to the officer's quarters.

"I want to see how you work. This is just part of the Quality control I do periodically with each of the cleaners," she had told the curious employees.

She carefully wrote down what was done and how each house was cleaned.

Alice stayed out of sight as she scoped out the security at the specified home. She noted the position of each of the guards and of the cameras in the house. She was not sure who lived there but it was clear they were important.

She knew the cleaning crew entered the base early in the morning and left late at night. This would give perfect cover for whatever was being planned.

Alice decided to handle the placement of the trucks.

"The fewer people in the mix the less chance of getting caught," she thought to herself.

Alice decided to take some additional action on her part. She would wait and watch the pickup and the return of her truck. Then she planned to bring the truck back to her fleet and remove the false bottom modifications. Perhaps this would make it harder to trace.

The fax number showed up by a bike messenger. The date of when and the location of where to put the vans came with the fax number.

Alice had found an industrial rental company that rented standard white vans. On the specified day she took a cab and got dropped off three blocks away. She walked into the rental place, gave a fake name, and showed a fake driver's license with a picture of some unknown woman and drove out with the truck.

After driving to the designated parking lot and leaving the keys under a brick she walked a few blocks away and took a cab to downtown and went into a store as if going shopping.

She figured she was being watched. She would be watching if she were forking out millions of dollars. She exited out another door and took a cab to within a few blocks of her business.

She then took her cleaning truck to the same parking lot and parked it next to the previous one. She put the keys under the brick. She had hoisted the bricks from an old brick pile along some industrial rail tracks.

She followed the same routine of going downtown by cab, going shopping and then she took a series of cabs and arrived within a block of her home.

Alice was ready to leave. She had everything she was planning to take put in a box at her office. She was traveling light.

Well before dawn Alice took her Styrofoam picnic box that she had filled with some sandwiches and drinks. She walked out and got into an old used car she had purchased in cash and drove to a small park with a picnic table from where she could observe the two vans.

"I guess these old opera glasses will finally prove to be of some use," she thought to herself as she looked through them to where the two trucks were parked.

She almost missed the pickup of her truck. Alice saw the lights come on and caught two people going into the back. One was a woman that looked a lot like her.

"They are going to try to implicate me. I am glad that I am planning to leave," Alice thought to herself.

"I have the rest of the day to wait. I know the house in question is the last in the cleaning route. It will be dark by the time they return.

It's time to go get my nails and hair done as scheduled. I will leave a generous tip so I will be remembered." Alice thought to herself as she departed the park.

Chapter 12: Kidnapped

The guy sweeping the floor gets a glance but never gets noticed. The bell hops cleaning tables mostly get ignored. The mowing crew comes in, surrounds a house, gets the lawn mown, the flower beds straightened out and leave. The homeowners would never have recognized any of them if they met them on the street. You, see the hotel the maids that come in make the bed vacuum the floor, replenish the shampoo, coffee bags but you would never recognize them anywhere else.

These are the invisible people. They are in plain sight, but they go unseen.

The cleaning van entered the base early in the morning and went to the base's PX where Starbucks was located.

There they bought a cup of coffee just like the normal cleaning crew always did.

"It must be nice working for a company that will buy you a cup of coffee each time you come to the base to clean houses," Max the driver of the van commented.

"Yea but I don't like the idea of having to clean houses all day long," Lester complained.

He was no sissy boy. He wanted only to do a man's kind of work.

"Lester, you are going to make more in one day than you have made all year. What's a few hours of house cleaning," Max said replied as he took a sip of his coffee?

"Matt and I agree with Max. A hundred grant a piece is a nice bonus. I don't mind vacuuming the rugs," Jason added.

Matt and Jason had been hired to be the muscle and enforcers. They would ride behind the transport truck as escorts.

Lester was the in the truck helper.

They finished their coffee and began their day of being housekeepers.

They knew that the action would happen at the last house.

Lydia, Darian, and Joe had become comfortable living in the house on General's row. They were guarded 100% of the time. Their guards were rotated about every other month. They had gotten to recognize most of them.

"I liked it better when we weren't considered important," Lydia commented as they were escorted back to the house. Every Friday the entire team shared a dinner at some local restaurant. The three of them had noticed the increased surveillance at these outings and they were now escorted wherever they went.

"Who would attempt to get us," Darian commented as they followed their escort up the stairs to the front door?

"Well, the General must think we are important to someone," Joe said as he greeted the guard at the front door.

Lydia walked in followed by Darian.

Joe hesitated. Something was not right. As he turned to look at the guard again, he saw the baton coming at him.

"Dam, you are slow," was the last thing he remembered thinking before the lights went out.

When he came to, he was sitting in a wheelchair with his wrists and ankles tapped to the handles. Lydia and Darian were restrained in a like fashion. They were in the back of a medium sized truck. It was outfitted with a couch, some beds and what looked like a Porto Potty.

"Let me look at that nasty gash. Sometimes I wonder at the stupidity of my team," the woman said as she carefully cleaned the encrusted blood from the gash over his eye.

"I need to put a couple of stitches in. You up for that, stud," she asked?

She was carefully threading a needle as she asked the question.

The movement of the truck had her swaying back and forth in front of Joe.

"Do I have a choice? Do you have any superglue," Joe asked?

He figured the gash could quickly and painlessly be closed by using super glue.

"Yeah, not really. Now hold real still," she said as she squeezed the gash shut and slowly made the first stitch.

Lydia watched as Joe silently endured the stitching. She was worried. He had been out for a long time. She was also impressed with his ability to take the pain and only flinch slightly.

"What do you want with us," Darian asked?

"Well, you all are the guinea pigs. Our customer wants to examine you to see if they can figure out the technology being used," she replied.

"And you will likely end up being dissected into tiny little pieces as well," she thought.

The challenge now would be to get them to the transfer site. Her team would only stop for gas. There was enough food to take them to their destination. The rendezvous site was across the border into Louisiana. Their goal was to look like any other plain delivery vehicle driving along the highway.

They would make a transfer to another team with a different vehicle once they crossed the border. That team would take the three on to the east coast.

"I am Brenda if you need anything call me. I will be back to feed you. You all behave back here," Brenda said as she opened a small door that went into the back of the driver's area.

"Is there any chance of using the toilet? We just got back home from a night out drinking, I am about to bust," Joe lied.

He wanted to get out of the chair and see if he could figure out some way to get free.

"I'll send Lester back. He is the one who whacked you. Don't mess with him, he has a mean streak in him," Brenda replied.

The three could hear Brenda telling Lester to let Joe go to the toilet and not to damage the goods any more than he had already done.

"You are a pain in my butt. Screw with me and I will do the other side. I don't care what Brenda has to say," Lester said as he made a point of tapping on Joe's wound above his eye.

Lester cut the duct tape on the ankles and then the wrists.

Joe just slumped in the chair and groaned.

He slowly stood up and rubbed his wrists. Lester had a knife in one hand and a police baton in the other.

"Now go do your thing. Go in and out slowly. Any messing around and I will put you down like a worthless dog," Lester threatened.

"Whoa, I feel a little woozy," Joe said as he faked a stumble.

Lester made only a small step in Joe's direction.

It was all Joe needed. Joe delivered a heel round house to the side of Lester's head. He then stepped in and hit him in the Adam's apple with his fingers. Lester let out a gurgle.

Joe then made a spin and brought his elbow into Lester's diaphragm. He was now standing with Lester behind him. He had both of Lester's arms clasped in his armpits. He took the knife and the baton and lowered Lester to the floor.

Joe made sure Lester was still breathing.

He quickly took the roll of duct tape and taped Lester's mouth shut. Then he taped his hands behind his back.

Lydia and Darian were both just looking at him, eyes in wide open surprise.

"Ssh, I am going to cut you lose but be very quiet. Let's see if we can get Brenda back in here," Joe whispered as he freed them.

"Hey, Brenda, get back here. This asshole puked on the floor," Joe called out trying to sound like Lester.

As Brenda came through the door, Joe pulled her into the back and closed the door. He put his hand over her mouth.

"You call out and I will break your neck," Joe threatened.

Brenda immediately began to cry out when he removed his hand. He hit her with the baton, and she went out.

"I warned her not to cry out. But I didn't break her neck," Joe said as Lydia gasped.

"Tape her into the wheelchair and tape her mouth shut," he instructed.

"I am going to take care of the driver. Let me go in first but come in right behind me. We need to keep the truck on the road.

I think there were more of them at the house. They may be escorting the truck. I will pull the driver out of the seat.

Lydia, you grab the wheel and Darian slip in and step on the gas pedal," Joe instructed as he put on Lester's ball cap and took off his belt.

"I should have hit him again," Joe mumbled in Lester's coarse style as he backed into the cab area.

When he turned the belt went immediately around the driver's throat and Joe pulled him backwards as Lydia went around and in on his left and Darian went around on the right.

The truck took a little turn but then straightened as Lydia held the steering wheel. Darian slid into the driver's seat and maintained the speed they had been going.

"Looks like Sam is getting tired," Jason who was the driver in the car behind the van commented.

"Well, I am sure Brenda will make sure that he keeps awake," Matt replied.

Joe kept pulling the driver until he was in the back. The driver was out cold. The belt around the neck had immediately made him pass out. Joe pushed on the driver's chest a couple of times until he could see that he was breathing. Then he taped his hands behind his back. And finally, he taped his ankles together.

Joe removed the tape from Brenda's mouth.

"You won't get away. You are being escorted. "And pay back is going to be hell," she spoke up from her wheelchair and spit in his direction.

"What are we going to do now," Lydia asked from behind him?

"We are going to get away of course," Joe said in a slow drawl and gave Lydia a smile.

"Do we know where we are? What highway we are on? How fast we are going and what time is it," Joe asked?

I have no clue where we are, but we are on US 10, doing sixty-five and it is four thirty in the morning," Darian replied.

"We want to get off at the next major truck stop. We need to do this at the very last moment so the escort car behind us can't follow. We need just enough time to get this truck out of sight among all the other trucks. Then we will either borrow a truck or a convenient car for the get away," Joe instructed.

"You mean we are going to steal a truck," Lydia said in amazement.

"Why not just go in and ask for help?"

"Yes, we could do that, but have you noticed that these guys are armed, somebody is likely to get killed," Joe replied.

"Hey, I like the idea of heisting a truck," Darian spoke up from behind the wheel.

"But do you know how to drive one of those beasts?"

"Yes, I do. We moved our cattle to the market via truck. I got lessons from our truck drivers every year," Joe lied.

He had gotten to drive a couple of times and knew how to manage the shifting. He hoped that if they took a truck, it would be a new automatic one.

"Truck stop ahead, get your seat belts on," Darian called out.

At the very last moment, so late that he had the truck on a skid and almost hit the off-ramp rail, Darian swerved and shot, full speed, up the off ramp.

He did not stop at the top but went straight across the small highway into a huge truck parking area. At this time of the early morning, the trucks were still parked in an orderly fashion.

Joe pressed Tom's telephone number and put the phone under the back seat.

"There between those two trucks. Put it just behind their cabs. Turn off your headlights. Turn off the engine. Lydia, grab some of the food Brenda mentioned. Let's move," Joe said as he opened his door and jumped out.

He crouched down and looked to either side under the trucks. About six trucks down there seemed to be a smaller one.

He dialed General Martinez's number and put the next phone down on the ground a few inches away from the back set of wheels of the semi he was under.

"Let's go to that small truck," he said quietly as he went under the first truck and then the next.

Out by highway, he thought he saw headlights coming into the truck stop.

"We have only a couple of minutes. Just follow my lead. We can't hesitate or delay.

When we get to the truck Darian you drive, Lydia, you help me. Do not race out of here but drive very slowly toward the gas pumps as if you are going to stop.

Lydia, you check for headlights out in the truck area. If they stop at the truck, we abandoned let me know," Joe's mind was racing.

They could not hope to outrun them down the highway, but they might be able to play a trick that he had learned as a teenager.

It turned out the vehicle he was targeting was not a truck but an RV.

The door came open with almost no effort. He was quickly inside and moved back to the bedroom. Darian got into the driver's seat and to his relief the keys were laying in the council area. He started the RV and slowly drove it toward the gas pumps.

"Easy, I don't want to hurt you. We are borrowing your RV to get away from some really bad guys. You will only have us around for about an hour. Then we will be off in some other direction," Joe said to the somewhat confused man coming out of the bedroom.

"OK, what do you want me to do," the man asked as he looked at Lydia?

"A beautiful Bonnie and a rugged Clyde," flashed through his mind.

"Let me give you our names and a number to call. Tell the person that answers that the mice are coming home," Joe replied as he scribbled down Linda's cell number.

"OK, what kind of trouble are you in," the man continued his inquiry?

"We have been kidnapped and are trying to get away from the kidnappers," Joe said quietly

"My name is Nancy, this is Fred. I heard what you just said. I believe you. Can I make you some coffee," Nancy asked?

"Well, that sounds really tempting but in the next few miles we may be doing some rather rough driving," Joe said.

They were now by the gas pumps. They were going behind the truck stop building. For a few moments they would be hidden from the trucks in the parking lot.

"Get on I-10 heading East. Once you get down the ramp get this RV going as fast as you can. "We need to get to the next exit and then head West," Joe said as he went up to Darian.

The sign put the next exit five miles way.

"Damn, I was hoping for a closer one," Joe said when he realized how close this was going to be.

"I am doing ninety-five. I didn't know these things could go that fast," Darian called over his shoulder.

"I didn't it know it could either," Fred replied as he sat down on the couch.

"Lydia, look out the back. Let me know if you see any headlights," Joe instructed.

"Do you folks have any weapons," Joe asked.

"We thought about getting a shot gun, but Nancy figured she might get scared one night and accidently shoot me. I figured we really didn't need one," Fred responded with a chuckle.

"One half mile to the exit," Darian called out.

"Turn off your headlights, slow down and take the ramp smoothly. Cross over and get the RV out of sight of the highway. I am going to jump out and monitor the road. Turn out all the lights and turn this rig around," Joe said as Darian slowed down to let him off after he had crossed over the overpass and was across the highway.

Joe trotted back to the highway and got there just when the escort car zoomed past. The kidnap truck came zooming by about thirty seconds later. The trick had worked.

He knew the next exit to the East was another seven miles down the highway. By then they would have figured out what had happened. He had about fifteen minutes to go West and get to the next truck stop and get a different vehicle.

When he got back to the RV, Fred was sitting behind the wheel.

"I had no clue how to turn this rig around," Darian commented when Joe looked at him.

"How fast do you want me to go," Fred asked.

"Well just about as fast as we got here. We need to get to the next truck stop and into a different vehicle," Joe replied.

"There is a truck stop one mile beyond the one where you high-jacked us. Will that do," Fred inquired with a chuckle?

"This is one trip Nancy, and I will remember for the rest of his lives," Fred said loudly as he stepped on the gas.

"When we get there, the best bet is for the three of us to go into the restaurant. I want to find out if there is a truck driver willing to take us to San Antonio," Joe said as he sat sideward in the passenger's seat.

"Nancy and Fred, you go back to the highway and head East. Get off after a couple of exits and have a nice breakfast," Joe suggested.

He had been trying to think how they could avoid a confrontation with the kidnappers.

"I hate to ask but do you have any money that you could loan us. Many truck drivers will take folks if they are willing to pay," Joe said.

He was only projecting what he had heard when he was younger.

"Sure, how much are you talking," Nancy asked?

"Would one hundred fifty dollars be asking too much," Joe said hesitantly.

"I will be right back," Nancy said as she went back into the bedroom. She returned with two fresh one-hundred-dollar bills.

"Don't have any fifties, will this do?"

"Thank you. Please give us your address and we will make sure you get it back," Joe said as he put the money in his pocket.

"This is the most fun I have had in years," Fred commented, "the exit is just ahead."

After getting good-bye hugs from Nancy and Fred, the three got out and watched the RV drive away.

Lydia was still carrying the bag of food that had remained untouched.

Chapter 13: Safe Return

People basically want to do good. Joe watched the RV drive away and thought about how two people awakened in their RV recovered from being themselves kidnapped to help three people escaping from their kidnappers.

How crazy could the situation get.

He thought about a herd of cows getting scared of a thunder bolt and taking off in a thundering, mindless flight across the prairie. He had ridden trying to gain control of such a herd. They had run until exhaustion finally brought them to a halt. He had no control. He had little effect in getting the herd to stop. He had been at the right place to guide them back to their original starting point.

Now he felt a little like the lead cow or steer at the head of the herd. Only the cowboys chasing them were not out to help them but to capture them.

Joe led the way into the truck stop restaurant where only a handful of people were sitting.

"Can I help you sweetie," a waitress with a name tag identifying her as Leatrice walked up with three well-worn menus.

"Yes, a table for three," Joe said as he looked around.

He walked up to the nearest person.

"You going to San Antonio," Joe inquired?

"Yup"

"Would you take three of us there," Joe went on.

"Nope"

"Try John at that table over there. He is running empty and could use a boost."

"Thanks," Joe said and looked over to a grey-haired man with a scraggly beard.

He was not sure about this guy, but he really had no choice.

"John, my name is Joe. My two friends over there and I are in need of a ride to San Antonio. The fellow over at that table said you sometimes take paying customers," Joe went immediately to the point.

"Did he now? Fifty bucks a head and eye candy sits in the passenger seat," John said in a rough voice.

Joe let out a chuckle.

"Just make sure you only look. I will throw in another fifty if we leave right now," Joe continued.

"Deal, do I have time to finish breakfast? And who are we running from," John asked?

"I will tell you on the way to San Antonio," Joe said as he got up.

"The money," John said with the question in the drawl?

"One hundred now and one hundred when we get there," Joe said as he flashed both hundred-dollar bills and put one bill on the table.

"Leatrice, I am sorry to have bothered you, but we need get going immediately.

If some rude people come in asking about us, please tell them you never saw us," Joe said as he got Lydia and Darian moving and following John out the door.

"See you next trip Leatrice," John said as he led the way to his truck.

As they got on the ramp going West, Joe saw the black car and the kidnap truck coming up the ramp from the East.

"The folks that are after us just drove into the truck stop," Joe announced.

"Now is a good time to tell me what you are running from," John said as he sped down the ramp and merged onto the interstate.

Joe started his explanation.

Meanwhile back in San Antonio, the two phone calls Joe had made, had put a rescue effort back on track.

"Linda just received a call from a couple that told her that the three mice are coming home," Tom said as he thought about the situation. This couple claims to have helped the three escape in their RV.

"Our first three human transmissions have been kidnapped. This was a well-planned kidnapping pulled off by experts. They took out our guards and then they took our three team members.

The guards are OK but will surely get hammered by their furious sergeant.

Joe must have put up a fight because we found his blood on the floor in the foyer.

We believe they were taken out by the East gate in a house cleaner's van. We are still trying to locate the van. Our folks have gone to the cleaner's home office and are examining the cleaning vans there. So far, they have not found anything. The cameras at the base gate got the license number of the van and it is getting a thorough examination.

However, unknown to the examiners, Alice had switched plates on her truck prior to delivering it and then switched the plates back afterwards. They were examining the wrong truck.

I dispatched three helicopter teams. One team is heading West, one team is heading East, one team is heading North.

There are four hilos per team.

We are going to get the bastards.

A few minutes ago, Tom got a call.

A moment later I got a call.

In both cases there was no one on the other end. Both phones are still on. We located where the phones are via GPS.

The team going East is in position. They are only a few moments away from the phone's locations. One phone is on the move in a westerly direction while the other is stationary.

I believe Joe, Lydia, and Darian somehow managed to escape from their captors and are on the run.

I hope we are in time to give them a hand," Jorge shared the situation.

This was as mad as he had ever been.

Back in the semi, Joe was sharing what he thought would be just enough to let John know he was helping the right people.

"The three of us are the successful subjects of a top-secret government experiment. I can't tell you any more than that or they will have to shoot you.

The folks chasing us are probably just doing it for the money, but they were intending to deliver us to the East coast. I figure some country like China, or Russia is hoping to examine us to see what they can learn," Joe explained.

"Well, I'll be dammed. I am in a real spy thriller. For thirty years I have imagined every cloak and dagger scenario as I drove my rig, now I am living a real thriller, Now this is it.

It's so much better than I ever thought it would be. Here I thought I was just going to give Miss Eye Candy and her two followers a ride home," John replied.

"My name is Lydia," Lydia said quietly but firmly.

She did not like being called "eye candy."

"Sorry, Lydia. I'm just an old Vietnam vet. I guess I let my manners slip," John apologized.

He had struggled to stay relevant for so many years. He was at one of the lowest points of his life and commiserating when Joe approached him. He had failed for more than a month to get any business for his truck.

"You all better fasten your seat belts. We have a black car zooming up behind us," John announced.

"You must be joking. These fellows have been watching too many movies," John said as the black car pulled in front of them and began to slow down.

John stepped on the gas, slammed into the car, and began to push it down the highway. The two vehicles began to pick up speed.

"This is Hilo one, we have a visual," the voice came out of the speakers as the Door team back at the base sat watching the big screen and the scene of the semi-truck pushing the car ahead of it.

Smoke was coming from the wheels of the car. A panel truck was coming up the left side of the semi.

"Watch this trick," John said as he turned the steering wheel left. The semi began to change lanes and the car in front spun out of control, rolled, and flipped into the ditch and went into a long slide on its top.

The panel truck tried to stop but it was pushed into the median. It bounced down the middle of the median. The driver over corrected and it turned over on its side and came to a sliding stop.

"Now that is what you can do with this rig if you know how to drive it," John said triumphantly.

"Yahoo, now that is my kind of driver," Tom said as he jumped up to cheer the driver.

"Where did they find this driver," Linda said as she joined Tom in his cheer?

"This is Hilo one, we have our men on the ground. The kidnappers are all alive, but we are going to need medical attention for most of them. Do you want us to stop the truck?"

"No, let them go on until they stop for gas. Sent one unit to escort them but follow slowly behind. Let's clean up the site. See if you can get the vehicles off the highway. I do not want this to get into the news," Jorge commanded.

"If I am not mistaken, I think we have picked up an escort. Look out your window and make sure it's a friend," John said as he looked over to Joe.

"Yes, it's one of ours," Joe said as he waved back to the helicopter and then sat back down.

When they saw Joe wave, every member of the team back at the base let out a cheer.

Jorge spent the next three days penetrating the security issue and writing his analysis. He ordered every individual in the program be re-certified and their security clearance re-examined.

Phil immediately began pouring over the security clearances of all the people involved in the effort. He shared with Elena that a large security issue had come up.

"It is time to disappear," Elena thought to herself as she listened to Phil.

She had sent in her most recent report when she had learned humans had successfully participated in the program. She figured the report had triggered the kidnapping.

She was aware of the next-door neighbor and his observation of her. She had found the listening devices and suspected he was there as the clean-up guy.

The observation car still came around periodically, and she knew they were connected to the US side. They were probably from homeland security or the FBI.

Elena was ready to leave. She went through the house and did a thorough sanitization. They would know a professional had done the work but all traces of her would be erased.

146

They would go to her bank. There they would find nothing about her that was real. Even her eye color was different when she went to the bank.

She had done a detailed cleaning of her car. She hated to leave it behind, but she had no choice. She had to clear out and leave nothing behind.

Elena walked up to the back door of the house next door and knocked on it. She carried a large briefcase in one hand and a two-wire stun gun in the other.

When the man inside opened the door, she shot him with the stun gun. The two darts hit him in the chest and delivered their shock. He went down and Elena pulled him away from the door and closed it.

She taped his mouth shut and then rolled him over and taped his hands behind his back and his feet together.

She went out back and returned with three large black trash bags loaded with all the items she needed to get rid of. Her trash bins were as clean as her house.

She looked around and found the car keys on the countertop. She then found her way to the garage. There was a dark blue Chevy parked in the garage. She put the briefcase down in the passenger seat and then put the trash into the trunk. She would drop each bag off at a different dumpster on her way out of the city.

She pulled on her black wig, put on her sunglasses, and pushed the button on the garage door opener. She backed the car slowly out of the driveway and drove in the opposite direction from where her other two observers were parked.

She drove out of San Antonio and headed north. She carried close to one hundred thousand dollars.

Her offshore bank account had over ten million in it. She was going to disappear for the next few months in the wild west.

She planned to travel and eventually she would surface somewhere in Eastern Europe or Southeast Asia.

It was time to start another life. She decided that she was officially out of the spy business.

Jorge sent in his report and awaited the summons to meet with President MacAdam.

And as expected, Jorge was summed, and he flew to Washington to meet with the President. He was made to cool his heals for over an hour as he waited to be escorted in to see her. He knew the wait was part of the game.

He was sure many people wanted his head on a platter. Even his wife had questioned the security of the project.

He was finally escorted in.

President MacAdam sat in one chair and Jorge sat in the other. He figured he would be lucky to remain in command of the Door project but unless ordered to do so he would not step down.

"Tell me how some group infiltrated our top-secret effort," President MacAdam said in a conversational tone?

She had read the detailed report the General had sent in and already knew the details. She wanted to hear the General speak.

She had to know if he was tough enough to be left in his current position.

Her team was for firing him.

She was not sure and planned to go with her gut.

"Madam President," Jorge began.

"Please call me Lacy," Lacy interrupted. She disliked the formality of the title.

"Yes, of course, Lacy," Jorge continued.

Jorge knew this was a character test. And it was a test he planned to pass. His passion for the Door program had become an absolute.

"Lacy, I take full responsibility for the Achilles Heel. Every person currently in our program and those recently recruited has gotten full top secret security clearances. They are each getting a review of this clearance. The first time we did not know of the healing aspect of our transmission process.

Somehow our transmission success was shared. This leak did not come from our team. It caused one family with a terminally ill child to succumb to a bribe of a million dollars," Jorge began.

The president was aware that the leak about the healing affect had been from some source outside of Jorge's team.

"I am aware of all of these actions, and I have a team investigating that leak.

Do you know that the FBI is currently investigating your security chief," the President asked?

"No, this is news to me," Jorge replied.

"What had Phil been up to," Jorge went through his mind.

"I will make sure they brief you before you return to San Antonio," President Macadam replied.

What would you do if all the countries agreed to collaborate and work together to open up the solar system," Lacy asked quietly?

"Well, that certainly would make the way forward a more open process. We would still need to keep our guard up to protect the health breakthrough we have achieved.

The healing aspect of this technology will upset every economy in the world. Every country will want to get their hands on it. I fear it could actually lead to riots as people all over the world seek its healing powers. I would however not want to share the details of our technology with these countries at this time," Jorge replied.

"I'm glad to hear you say that. I do not want anyone to learn how to transmit. The transmission-receive units for the Door project are almost complete.

Our three "Door Ships" I believe you gave them this name are ready for space assembly.

I am going to offer rides out to the solar system for the Door people of each participating country.

We will incorporate these door men and women, but we will remain in control of the technology for as long as possible," Lacy replied.

"Tomorrow, I will meet with the Chinese ambassador and lodge a formal complaint about the kidnapping. All of our intelligence indicates they were the ones behind this attempt. They will of course deny having anything to do with it. I would not expect anything else, but it will soften them up for the offer of cooperation.

This offer will be made by our UN representative, in the coming week," the President shared.

"That is a very smart move," Jorge replied.

He was still wondering what Phil had been up to. Phil was his trusted security chief. Was he the leak?

"Tell the young man named Joe that if it was possible, I would give him a metal for his heroic action," Lacy said as she indicated their meeting was over.

"I guess I still have my job," Jorge said as he stood up.

"Yes, but make sure you keep it all together. This effort must be a success. I have used all my connections to make this happen. I don't have the luxury of starting over with someone new," Lacy said as the door opened.

Jorge was escorted out by one of the aids as Larry Madden the UN ambassador came into the room.

"Well did you fire him," Larry asked as he watched the General leave?

"No, the General responded exactly as he should have, and he continues to demonstrate a passion for the work he is doing. I will fire him if he does not fire his security chief when he finds out what has transpired," the President continued.

"Now let's talk about your report to the UN and the request for global co-operation. I have set up a meeting with the Chinese ambassador prior to the UN session. It's time we play hard ball with our Chinese competitors," President Lacy commented as she turned her attention to the next step of getting the opening of the Solar System for the entire world.

Back in San Antonio with the door team, Jorge announced his survival as the leader of the door team.

"I survived. I am sure my name is at the top of the list of Generals to terminate if one more thing goes wrong," Jorge shared with the team.

"Joe, the President wanted me to tell you that if she could, she would give you a medal for your brave actions," Jorge continued.

"Well, thanks, but I was just trying to save my skin," Joe answered.

"Well, Joe is a hero to me," Lydia said as she winked at Joe.

"Our security Chief has been replaced. He has been involved with a questionable person who has disappeared.

The FBI believe his companion was a spy for one of the competing countries.

Next door to his companion's home they found a bound and gagged individual. This individual turned out to be a known assassin. The person who got away is a professional as well. She knew about the guy next door and there is not a trace of her existence in the house or at any of the places she frequented.

I have chosen Phil's deputy to replace him in the short term," Jorge shared with the team.

He had talked to Phil immediately after leaving the President's office and had asked him to stand down until he was cleared of wrongdoing.

"What wrongdoing are you talking about," Phil had fired back. He still did not know that Elena had made her departure.

"My god, I was the leak," Phil had exclaimed when Jorge shared the details he had learned from the FBI.

He immediately declared his resignation. He knew that he faced serious charges. He told Jorge that he would contact legal. Jorge smiled and politely told Phil that he was under arrest and that he would indeed get a lawyer to represent him, but he would be cooling his heels in the brig.

Jorge had then gone to update his team on the events that were about to transpire.

"The President is going to offer to unify the Door effort into a global program. Tomorrow, I will be flying to the Cape to meet with the Brazilian team. The Brazilian's have already offered to participate with us so I will immediately invite their scientists and their Door candidates to join us here in San Antonio.

I am sure that the Russians will join us since they have indicated they will support the unification proposal.

The Chinese are the most likely group to have organized the kidnapping.

The President is going to use the kidnapping as leverage to get them to support her proposal.

The only key hold out is India and the President hopes to buy their support.

She is leveraging everything she can to get this to happen.

As far as I know, our team is the only one that has the capability to transmit and receive humans. In fact, our intelligence indicates that none of the other countries have successfully transmitted any living animal or plant," Jorge said as he looked around at the team the team.

"How are you planning to integrate their science team," Linda asked.

She was thinking about how to protect their scientific lead.

"I would like you, Tom, Aaron, and Jacqueline to determine how we can bring in the scientists of all the countries and still maintain technical secrecy. We are not to divulge the life-saving attribute it carries with it," Jorge instructed.

"Joe, Darian, Lydia, and Ryan, I would like you to design a program to train all the Door volunteers. I will add a couple of more members to your team. They will be experts in training people for the space program.

Your team will need to learn how to assemble the Doorships out in space.

The volunteers will come from all over the world. There will most likely be around fifty candidates.

Eighteen will be selected to deliver the Doors.

The others will likely be made part of the exploration teams that will utilize the Doors to explore our solar system," Jorge continued assigning people to new roles.

He knew the speed of implementation would increase in the near future.

Chapter 14: The Chinese Competitors

Advances come in surges that follow years of toil by multitudes of developers competing to be the first to reach the breakthrough goal.

The steam engine, the first car, the telegraph, and the radio each had a long developmental history before the success barrier was broken.

The current race to conquer matter transmission followed a similar but more intense competitive path.

The technology had advanced to a level where the lay person was left far behind and in ignorance.

Even the leaders of most countries had no clue how to evaluate the success or failure of their efforts. All wanted to see what the other country was doing.

The spy business became lucrative as a few million here and there meant almost nothing if new information could be attained.

Jeffrey Yang was in a deep pit. He was in trouble.

His top scientists had not been able to recombine living tissue. They had transmitted a command signal that produced blobs of organic material, but they had little to do with the goal of transmitting and recombining an animal let alone a human. The leaders did not seem to care how to get the transmit to happen. They were willing to take as much risk as necessary to be successful and be able to move out into the solar system faster than the other competing nations. The lives of their volunteers were secondary.

"I am likely to be shot," Jeffrey thought as he reviewed the latest progress report. It basically said his scientist didn't have a clue of what to do next. He had written it in as positive a tone as possible but there was no way to disguise failure.

His grape vine informed him that the US had successfully achieved human transmission. He had also heard about a failed attempt to kidnap the three people that had experienced the Fold transfer.

To Jeffrey this was an indication of how desperate his leaders were to get this technology. They had most likely arranged for the kidnapping in hopes of learning how the technology operated. He knew that the three would provide little value about how the process to transmit and receive worked.

"I am glad for the people being kidnapped that the attempt failed. They would have ended up in my hands. I know the pressure would have been on to examine them even to the point of doing autopsies on them," Jeffrey thought to himself.

He had no illusions as to how far he would be pressed to get results.

That morning he had said goodbye to his wife and child as he did every day with the anticipation of never seeing them again.

The entire program was on track except for the transmission break through. The spaceship and its crew would be ready.

Jeffrey knew that there was not going to be a Chinese transmit-receive unit on them.

Jeffrey had attended the Ohio State University in the US for a master's in business administration.

One of the places he had visited was the Air Force Flight Museum in Dayton, Ohio. There he had seen the models of jet planes designed in the thirties before the engines to propel them had been invented. The designers had defined the need for the next generation of engines. It took the breakthrough by the jet engine designers to finally provide an engine to power the planes.

This was the situation his program was currently experiencing. They had built all the hardware, trained their people but did not have the heart of their program. They did not have transmit-receive and reconstruct capability.

They did not have the equivalent of the jet engine.

The intelligent agency, or spy network had sent word of the US success. The US appeared to have made the breakthrough.

"How in the world had their scientists figured it out?

Ours have the same training, are just as smart. How did we miss it," flashed through Jeffrey's mind?

He had discussed this with everyone on his team and none of them had any new ideas.

He had been summand for a "*discussion*" with some of the top government leaders. He thought of his beautiful daughter and wondered if he would see her that evening.

He was picked up in a black Mercedes limo and driven to the meeting site.

He was escorted through the wide well-lit hallway into a room with a long meeting table. Only two seats remained. He was guided to the single seat at the other end of the table.

"Gentleman," he said in formal greeting as he was led to his seat.

Just as he sat down the door opened and when he looked up to his surprise Le Cho Wei, their current party leader entered and sat at the other end.

This, Jeffrey knew, was much more than an update.

"This is more serious than I thought," flashed through his mind.

"I understand that our scientists have not been able to achieve the breakthrough on the material transmission capability we have been seeking," Wei said quietly.

"That is correct. They have tried very hard to achieve that breakthrough.

I take full responsibility for not having achieved what we so desperately seek," Jeffrey replied.

He had come prepared to assume all blame. He did not want to get his scientist's shot. One person would be enough.

He just wished it did not have to be him, at least not today.

"A proposal has been made to us by the US and its allies in the United Nations to make the effort to open the Solar System, a global effort. Should we accept this offer," Wei inquired?

Jeffrey wanted to shout an immediate, YES, but thought for a rather long time before answering. He looked at the stern, stoic faces lining each side of the table. They all appeared to want his head.

In this case the truth might be his executioner, but a lie would result in the same execution within a few weeks. He saw no safe path and chose to take the most truthful one.

"I believe we should agree to participate. We are not making any progress in our ability to transmit detailed enough instructions to recombine a life form," Jeffrey replied.

They also did not have the ability to transmit an object. A shiver went down his back. He felt that the next few moments would determine his fate.

A picture of his wife and daughter laughing on the beach flashed through his mind. He wished he had a god to shield him.

"What is the barrier to our progress?

The US team seems to have made that breakthrough," Wei inquired?

There seemed to be a general shaking of heads in the room indicating they all wanted to know why their team was losing.

"I have spent many sleepless nights wondering about this.

I have met with our scientist and had many discussions. They have spent countless hours working together and separately trying to understand what we are missing.

When our intelligence indicated the US team had a breakthrough, our team reviewed every concept again. It is now clear that our efforts were not sufficient, and we cannot explain what we missed. If we could define our barrier, my team would break through it," Jeffrey replied quietly.

"Now I will be led out and disappeared," he thought to himself.

"We will accept the proposal for a Global effort. You will return to your team and determine who on the team will participate in the US effort.

There will be a meeting in a month to organize the Global effort. It is your responsibility to get appropriate representation and recognition of our contribution to this Global effort. I desire that China gets the appropriate good position as we contribute significantly to the effort.

The proposal includes the invitation to send three candidates to the US in the next month. Are we able to meet this timing," Wei inquired?

Jeffrey was surprised at the level of detail the invitation included. It could only mean that the breakthrough was indeed real.

"Yes, we have nine candidates in training and will select the three best ones.

We also have our space vessels almost ready to launch. We should leverage our very substantial launch capability.

I will personally bargain for a strong position and more representation," Jeffrey replied.

He felt a weightlifting from his shoulders. It seemed he would see his wife and daughter this evening.

Jeffrey was escorted out of the meeting room and driven back to his office.

His team members knew he had been called in and were waiting to hear of their fate.

Fang Zhin Xiao was leading her two partners as they took their daily ten-kilometer morning jog. She was to be the female member of a three-person crew.

He-Ping Ye was the calm, levelheaded mathematics wizard. He was the counterbalance to Sheng Zang whose specialty was biology and who was super intense and competitive.

"What do you think the meeting this afternoon is about," He-Ping vocalized?

"Well, there doesn't seem be any progress in the ability to transmit and reconstruct any living thing. So, we will probably hear about the end of the program or a change in the leadership of the program," Sheng replied.

"I heard a rumor that the West has made a proposal to make this effort a global effort," Fang Zhin threw out what she had learned from an associate in the security agency.

"Then it should be an interesting meeting," He-Ping commented.

"I hope Jeffrey survives this morning's leadership meeting," Fang Zhin commented.

"Me too, I would hate to have to deal with a new leader," Sheng commented.

He had struggled to remain quiet and appear humble in front of the current leaders. He was forever mumbling snide remarks about their incompetence to himself.

"I have also heard that the West has made the breakthrough that has eluded our scientist," He-Ping replied.

"I hope so because I do not want to come out like the fish and mice our scientist have been trying to transmit," Fang Zhin commented as she thought about the blobs that had been produced at the reconstruction chamber.

Jeffrey had been very relieved to have been brought back to the team's work center after the morning meeting.

Later that afternoon he called a meeting of all the current Transmission-Reconstruction team members.

"We are entering a new phase in our efforts to transmit and recombine living matter.

I would like to announce that we will be working with a global team on this effort. We will be partnering with scientists from all over the world. They are seeking out our expertise and our vital human and equipment resources.

This expanded effort will be known as the Qin Yuchi-Door program," Jeffrey announced to his team.

At least that would be what it would be called by his team.

"In other words; we have hit the wall and are now willing to work with the West to see if we can understand what breakthrough they have achieved," Sheng commented quietly to his two partners.

Sheng was the rebellious one of the team. He disliked being constantly watched and controlled.

"Or better yet, we will be working in the US and be able to go to Disney World and Universal Studios," Fang Zhin quipped in response.

"Is that in California or Florida," He-Ping chimed in?

Chapter 15: Unification

Jorge knew that the strength of a team came from its diversity and a focus on a single goal. Strong, supportive leadership provided the nurture that allowed a team to form, coalesce, and grow and in designing the work so leaders overlapped and collaborated to create a hands-on culture.

Jorge had led his HR team through an organizational design to establish a metanoic organization and culture. This he knew was the quickest way to accelerate the Door effort, to challenge all those involved and to make it a desirable and fun place to work

He had personally picked the people and put them in the roles he felt they would perform best. He really wanted a win for everyone.

Once the agreement to make the Door program into a global effort was agreed to, Jorge had recruits arriving from around the world. The most recent recruits from the US team had been contacted and had agreed to be a part of the team.

One of his prize recruits was driving excitedly back from the post office on a small highway in Vermont.

Samantha was speeding down the highway. She had fulfilled her parents dream when she graduated with a Chemical Engineering. That had been her parents' dream for her. Her dream for herself was in the letter she had gone to town to get. The job offer in the letter was her dream job for herself. Her dream had come true, and she was eager to share it with her parents.

She had kept this a secret from them and now she was ecstatic and wanted to share it.

Her parents ran a small apple orchard, and their maple trees yielded enough sap to produce maple syrup for sale. The income from the orchard and maple syrup had never amounted to more than spending money.

Her parents also ran a bed and breakfast. The rental from it during the spring to fall cycle added enough for the family to live on.

Even then the main income had come from her father's small engineering practice.

Her parents had met in college. Her mother was Vietnamese and her father a Vermont native with roots back to the early colonists.

They had met, fallen in love, and married while in college. Mom claimed she had only done so because she felt sorry for Dad.

Dad always told of seeing the woman of his dreams and pursuing her until she said yes to his proposal. It was clear to all that the two were not only in love but the best of friends.

Samantha was an only child. Her best friend, Beth, lived on the giant apple orchard that bordered her parent's twenty-acre orchard. Beth's parents had twenty acres of apple trees and forty acres of maple trees and maybe another five acres of garden and ten acres of grass land.

Samantha's garden provided a year-round supply of potatoes, fresh tomatoes in the summer and canned tomatoes through the winter, squash, pumpkin, cucumber, and pickles and during the season, sweet corn. Their garden provided the family sustenance.

Their grocery expenses were minimal.

Samantha had a love-hate relationship with the garden. She hated the work, but she loved eating what it provided. The family always worked on the garden together. In the spring they would spend an hour every evening first preparing the garden, then planting the small plants and seeds. Then they would do the weeding. She had many fond memories of this time together. There was always a constant dialogue on different topics.

The garden it turned out was the one thing she missed while attending the U of M. Her room at college ended up full of spice plants like basil and rosemary. She was known as the spice lady. Since she also grew habaneros peppers, she made her name the *"Hot spice girl."*

The grassland, on the farm, was where the two milk cows, a few sheep and goats were kept.

It was also the place where Samantha spent many an hour laying in the grass looking at the clouds, dreaming of space, and imagining traveling to the planets in the solar system.

She could only remember good times at home.

In High School she had experienced some hassle because of her mixed heritage. However, she was in the top of her class. This had put her in the elite crowd, and she had many good friends. Her good looks and her membership on the cheer leading team made her known to all.

She was active in the school paper and had tutored those needing help.

She had always ranked in the top five of her class and had earned the top spot by one hundredth of a point just prior to graduation. She had laughed about the huge margin by which she had won.

She had applied to numerous schools and had received at least a half a dozen scholarship offers. She had selected the University of Michigan. It featured a rich academic slate, and it was far enough away to meet her criteria of becoming independent.

Her first year was really difficult. She missed Beth, her best friend. Beth had chosen to go to Brown University in Boston. This had been Samantha's second choice, but it was much more expensive, and they had not offered what U of M offered.

The U of M had offered her a full scholarship, a computer, and a small stipend. They had her with the computer but cinched it with the stipend.

The engineering program at U of M was one of the tops in the nation. Samantha went at it with full energy and was soon recognized as one of the top students in the Engineering Program.

In her final semester, the dean of the school, Dr. Samuel Trimble, approached her and suggested she apply to the Air Force Academy to the Door program and get a master's degree in Space Science.

"What in the world is a Door program," Samantha asked when he mentioned it?

"I can't tell you much about it. Well really nothing about it since I don't know what it is about. But my best friend is a professor there and he asked me to keep a look out for some top talent. He claims it is a program that will change the world as we know it," Dr. Trimble replied.

She had applied. She had turned down several top job offers once she had decided to apply at the Air Force Academy.

She had not shared this decision with her parents and felt guilty about it. She had been nervous about her decision.

If she were not accepted, she would need to get a job as soon as possible. Such a delay would put her at the end of the job selection list with most companies.

Most of her classmates were boasting about the great job offers they had received and accepted. She had interviewed a some of the same companies but had let the companies know that she was planning to get a master's degree.

Since coming home from school, she had made the daily trip into town to check on her post office box.

The acceptance letter had arrived this morning. She had been waiting when it was put into her mailbox. It was hard for her to hold the speed limit. She could not wait to tell her parents the good news.

Her mother had been probing to find out what was going on, but she was still enjoying the fact that Samantha had been the valedictorian of her class.

Her father had been more direct.

"When are you going to tell us what you have going on," he asked her?

"I will know in a few days. Then I will tell you and Mom," Samantha had replied.

She had given her Dad a hug and whispered, "It's a great opportunity, I just don't know if I will be accepted."

Now she was rushing home to do just that.

"Yes, yes, yes, yes," kept going through her mind. She did not know why but she had become convinced that her acceptance into the Door program was a pivotal point in her life.

The acceptance letter on the passenger seat was from The United States Air Force Academy. The academy was just north of Colorado Springs. She was going West.

Jorge had directed the recruiting be done through the Academy. The location was intended to throw off anyone trying to determine who was being recruited for the Door program. A receiving team would meet the new recruits as they arrived at Colorado Springs and then after a brief registration as graduate students, they would be transferred to the San Antonio Air Base.

Samantha was going to live her dream.

Meanwhile in the other side of the country in Oregon, Harold Hatfield Hensley, who was known to his friend either as H or H cubed was enjoying his brief return home.

He was walking the beach covered with the logs that were washed up by the storms. These logs had escaped from the thousands of logs that were floated along the coast on their way to the sawmills.

Lincoln City was a quiet place. It attracted many summer tourists, but it was not a tourist destination. It had a faithful set of people that came back every year.

Then there were a few tourists who after listening to their friends talk about how enjoyable it was, would decide they too should check out the area. Word of mouth provided all the tourists the small city could handle.

It attracted those folks who liked to walk the beach versus swim in the ocean.

His father was a self-employed plumber. His mother was a waitress at the Dotti Restaurant.

He was the first in the family to go to college.

H cubed had gone to Taft High School and the school's four R's; Relationships, Respect, Responsibility and Resilience had given him much of his guidance.

His parents encouraged his scholastic efforts. They had both barely finished High School before they went to work.

They gave him all the support he needed. They wanted the best for him.

He was a starting end on his football team and his parents were always in the stands rooting him on. Basketball was not for him, but he was on the baseball team.

He lettered in both sports.

H cubed spent two years going to the Oregon Coast Community College. He could not afford the cost of most colleges and he was not going to put his family on the spot.

He planned to work and get as much at the community college as possible and then try to get into one of the leading Universities.

He continued to apply to all the top name universities.

To his surprise and his parents' jubilation, he received a two-year scholarship to Dartmouth. He had submitted an application to an obscure program dealing with matter transmission. He had postulated that matter did not need to actually be transmitted but needed to be assembled from material at the receiving end.

The scholarship was actually from the US Navy. He would need to join the Navy and would graduate as an Ensign. He was clueless on how the Navy had gotten involved in matter transmission, but it was an easy decision. They would pay his tuition and they paid him as a student. He would be obligated to serve at least two years in the Navy.

He loved the Ocean, so it was a good fit.

Dartmouth was a surprise to H. It was located about two hours northwest of Boston. The countryside reminded him a lot of home. For the first time he had a small income that he could enjoy. He was practical but he made it a point to try all the eateries around the campus.

The theoretical education was intense and somewhat of a shock to him. H had never studied so hard. He had been in the top of his high school class.

He was on the Dean's honor list at the Community College. He realized it would be harder to maintain that standing at Dartmouth.

Suddenly he felt disoriented and poorly prepared. The program designed especially for the Navy, ran eight hours a day, five days a week and it had enough homework that the entire weekend was spent studying. He was struggling to keep up for the first time in his life.

The other students in his group were as rattled as he. Several dropped out and chose a less intense program.

H was determined to be the best in his class. He went into hyper drive. He aced every quiz, every test, and every paper. He studied relentlessly. His personal life was a zero, but his academic side was superb.

Then one day he was called in.

"This is General Jorge Martinez of the US Air Force," his professor said in introduction.

H came to attention and saluted the general as he had been taught by his ROTC leader. He had no clue how to act around a General.

"At ease," the General said as he returned the salute.

"I am here to make you an offer to participate in one of the greatest adventures you could possibly wish for," General Martinez came right to the point.

"A team is being assembled that will change the course of human history. I am not in a position to tell you what this team will do. I can tell you that only a handful of people will be made this offer. The team will come together at Colorado Springs.

Your theory of matter transmission and your performance caught our attention. You must make your decision today.

Let's go to lunch and then afterwards you can tell me what you have decided."

H looked over to his major professor.

He got a raised eyebrow and these words, "I am a scout for the Door program. They are seeking the best of the best; those who rise up to the challenge. You were the only candidate I submitted. I suggest you take the offer."

H went to lunch, he listened to the General and he took the offer.

He was now home for a brief couple of weeks. He had explained to his parents as best he could what he would be doing. He informed them that he would be in a special program. At worst he would receive a master's degree. At best he would be part of a secret program that was supposed to change the world.

It was only a short time later when he sat in a gym and listened to his new boss.

Jorge and his team sat on an elevated platform in the gym they had converted as their main gathering location. What had seemed like endless negotiations with all the countries around the world had concluded and Jorge had obtained the control he wished to have.

Each of the leaders of the competing door programs were with him on the platform. The first three rows on the gym floor were the seats for all the new Door candidates. Behind them sat the team of scientists and support personnel now making up the program team.

"Welcome to all of you. Our program has been named the Por-Qin Yuchi-Door program. For all of us in this room, we will simply call it the Door program," Jorge began his opening remarks.

He had become tired of the negotiations over the official name of the international program. In the end the language used in the name covered three quarters of the people in the world.

"Well at least Jeffrey got our program name included. Good for him," Sheng whispered in Chinese to his two partners.

Jorge made the point that there were sixteen countries contributing participants. Each of these countries had one representative on the leadership team. Jorge had specifically limited them to act as an advisory and progress audit team. They had no say in what their specific candidates would do.

He maintained complete control of all day-to-day activities of the program. This was a hard-fought agreement. He was probably the only one satisfied with the outcome.

"You are a tougher and better negotiator than I had expected," President MacAdam had praised him during his now weekly meeting with her.

"It's not that hard to negotiate when you hold the winning hand and know it," Jorge had replied.

He and his original team were all pleased with the control they all maintained.

"Let me be the first to bow down in humble apology for ever doubting our red headed genius," Jacqueline had said when she learned that they were the only team to have successfully achieved true transmission and reconstitution.

Tom was just about to give a sarcastic reply when Linda bobbed him on the back of the head and said, "Just say thank you."

"Thank you," Tom had dutifully replied but there was a twinkle in his eye and his face turned red.

"Let me introduce the leadership team for this program. Each will come to the podium and give a brief introduction," Jorge continued.

Chapter 16: The Dark Side of Politics

Lacy had no illusion about who her enemies were and where they sat. One of her staunchest enemies sat in her cabinet. She had shared with her husband that seeing Mathew Pinkerton try to hide his distain and the pain he felt because he had lost to her gratified her immensely. She was not a vindictive person, but she relished the fact that someone as distorted in his values as Mathew Pinkerton was being kept out of the game. He was always in her view.

Mathew Pinkerton's life changed during that first meeting where the cabinet had discussed the implications and ramifications of the Door's ability to transmit the human and to simultaneously cure cancer.

He left the meeting in what he would later understand as an absolute hate trance. He sat for hours secluded in his office.

"How can I destroy her project and her career?" was all that would go through his mind.

He realized he had an absolute hate for the person who was President. He should have been President and she should have been sent home to be an old busy body.

He still could not get over the fact that she had somehow been selected over him.

He had been even more surprised when she won the election over her presidential rival. He had been sure she would lose.

"Will see that bitch go down in flames," Mathew thought to himself as elements of a plan came into his mind.

"I have connections that even she cannot find out about," went through his mind as he thought about his Russian and terrorist connections. These connections could be utilized to get the fire power he would need.

They would be brought together in a way that would satisfy the Russians and the radical ISIS leaders.

His upcoming trip to Russia to discuss joint military maneuvers would provide him the cover he needed to put into place the long-term part of the plan he had formulated.

A second meeting with Arabic leaders of the Middle East to discuss US military assistance provided the backdrop to connect the Russian part of the plan to the execution part of the plan.

Mathew wasted no time in setting up his clandestine meetings. The next meeting took place in Egypt.

Muhyi had been captured and brought to Egypt in hopes he would provide information that could be used to strike back at the ISIS leadership. The intense interrogation effort was finally abandoned when it was clear they could not break the man's will.

Mathew forged the paperwork that authorized the release of Muhyi al Din Hakimi on behalf of the United States.

He then arranged to brief him and then have him transported back to the ISIS territories.

Mathew offered Muhyi missile launch capabilities in exchange for one specific action. Muhyi smiled as he accepted an offer he would gladly carry out.

Mathew then activated his next plan. The move to provide distraction and irritation only took him a phone call. He went to the hardware store and bought a prepaid phone. He placed a call and gave detailed information about the location of the Door program. He arranged for demonstrations at the Lakland Air Base.

This action was intended to eat up valuable security resources. It would hinder the work of the Door team, but Mathew knew it would not stop its momentum.

He just wanted those involved in the Door program to be uncomfortable and irritated and to be somewhat slowed down.

"Dad always said to have plans A, B, and C to accomplish an important task," Mathew thought to himself as he thought about what he was doing.

He still had two more plans he wanted to put into place.

He knew what plan B needed to be, but he didn't know how to put it into action. He would keep his eyes open to see how it might be executed, he thought to himself as he stepped out of his shower.

He had come home and had dinner with his wife and then had put in two hours on the treadmill. It was when he sped up for a higher speed run and had run out of breath that the idea had popped into his mind.

"What's so funny," his wife of more than forty years asked when she heard his laughter.

"Nothing dear, just something that happened in the office today," he had replied.

But it was something.

He now knew what plan C would be.

The next morning as he was shaving, he looked at the strange man smiling back at him from the mirror and wondered who he was.

"Boo," he said into the mirror. In a flash plan B came to life.

"Boom" he said into the mirror: "Boom, boom, boom"

He did not recognize the crazed man looking out from the mirror.

"Well, the devil will have my soul, but I will have a few years of sweet revenge," Mathew thought to himself.

In the following weeks he finalized the details of plan A and he continued to work out how he would execute plans B and C.

He wished he could utilize more of the power he wielded as Secretary of Defense, but that avenue was not available for the clandestine actions he needed to take.

For plan C he contacted a group in Kenya that he had utilized in a counter insurgency campaign a few years before. They had later become adversaries, but he was still able to connect and get them interested in what he had in mind.

He worked with a long times arms dealer to deliver the weapons and telescopes that plan C required. The final part of plan C remained open. He did not know how he would execute the placement of the explosives that needed to be put into place.

"I will need to find out who the key persons are to be able to finalize the actions of both plan B and C," Mathew thought to himself.

He hoped the search for the key people would be successful.

The heat of summer was winding down and the cooler autumn weather was a great relief. Jorge was pleased to see everything settle down.

The entire officers housing area was now used by the expanded Door team.

Colonel Sylvester Sloan, the original security officer of the program had resigned when he realized he was the source of the leaks leading to the kidnapping of the Joe, Lydia, and Darian. He was soon to go on trial.

He was currently working with the FBI seeking to find the disappeared Elena. He knew he had been used and was compelled to find her. It was not a matter of revenge because he really still felt he loved her, but it was a matter of honor.

She had used him, and he felt she should be accountable for her illegal behavior.

Jorge's new security officer, Doug Hasterly, was taking no chances.

The housing area was cordoned off with a razor wire topped fence and guards patrolled continuously around the perimeter. There was only one access gate into this inner area.

The main perimeter around the entire base had been beefed up.

This ensured there were two layers of security guarding the Door personnel.

Off base activity was kept at a minimum and anyone going off the base was driven, escorted, and had a protective detail assigned to guard them.

Movement on the base was less obtrusive but the escorts were always within visual distance.

Doug didn't know it, but it turned out to be the calm before the storm.

As Joe went out on his jog, he said hello to the person at the gate to the inner perimeter.

His morning run took him by the main gate as he followed the chain link fence back around to the inner gate and to the house that he, Darian, and Lydia were still sharing.

The signs the protestors were waving on the other side of the fence made it immediately obvious that the word about reconstitution had leaked out.

You can't play GOD, you will all go to HELL, and "Let the Prisoners Go" was on one poster with razor wire as a frame were just a few of the signs the demonstrators were waving.

Joe cut short his jog and hustled back to the house to get his camera.

"Where are you going with your camera," Lydia asked when she saw that Joe seemed to have some sort of mission in mind?

"I am going to take some pictures of people and cars. There is a major demonstration being organized at the gate," Joe replied.

"Wait for me," Lydia shouted after him as she put her breakfast bowl into the sink and ran out after Joe.

Joe approached the driver of the van that the team always had available to them and asked to be driven to a mound with a memorial marker that was about a half a block from the main gate.

"This puts us in a great vantage point for photos," Joe said to Lydia as he set up his tripod.

Joe made it a point to first get photos of all cars that had visible license plates.

Then he methodically zoomed in on each person and took a close up of the face, and then he took a total body shot.

He then took additional photos of every car.

Finally, he zoomed in on each placard and got a clear picture of them.

"I think I have everything here. Let's go take a look at the other two gates," Joe instructed their driver.

Each gate turned out to have a few people and once again Joe made a point of getting a set of photos with all the details he could think of.

"Now let's go see Doug and find out where these folks are from. There were plates from many states but a common plate at each gate was from Mississippi. I think that will lead to us in finding out how these folks knew to be here," Joe commented.

"Why is that important," Lydia asked?

"Someone leaked the information.

Jorge's head will be on platter if this situation gets blamed on any of us," Joe replied as he replaced the SD card in his camera with a new blank one and put the one with the pictures in his wallet.

He was taking no chances with someone taking his SD card. He knew he had vital information on it.

The staff at Doug's office was just arriving when Joe and Lydia walked in. It was a Saturday, but security had become a seven-day work week.

"We would like to see Doug," Joe said as they stopped outside of his office where his secretary guarded the door.

"He just got in and there seems to be some problems. Can you come back later," she asked as she looked at her screen as if she was looking for an open time slot on the calendar.

"No, he needs the information I have about this problem, and he needs it now," Joe said as he walked past her desk and opened the door.

"I'm with him," Joe heard Lydia say as he stepped into Doug's office.

"I'll call you right back," Doug said as he put down his phone.

"I gave instructions that I was not to be disturbed," Doug began in a somewhat angry voice.

Doug was a large imposing figure at any time.

When he got angry his face turned red and his appearance would have frightened a mad dog.

Joe took several steps toward him closing the gap to within arm's length. They were eye to eye. Lydia thought there might be a fight.

"I figured as much, and your support did her best to keep me out.

However, I have the photos of all the license plates of the cars outside the gate and of all the people as well.

Assign one of your analysts to me and we can do a search of where these people are from, who owns the cars and who is connected to whom.

"We can get this done in short order and you will have the information you and Jorge will need," Joe said in rapid fire as he leaned into toward Doug.

Lydia thought about her brother, half the size of her Dad facing off against each other in an argument.

"I will do better than that. You have the entire staff at your disposal. Let's go out there and get them organized. I need this done yesterday," Doug said as his face returned to a normal color, and he put his arm on Joe's shoulders.

He then led the way out into the office.

"Everyone, listen up. There are demonstrators at all our gates and the crowd is growing. We need to find out who is behind this action and how they learned about this location.

Joe has some license plate pictures and pictures of all the demonstrators that are out there at the moment. I want each of you to take a plate and run it down and I want everyone remotely connected with the owner of each car to be identified.

And I mean everyone, mothers, fathers, sisters, brothers, aunts, uncles, cousins, and great grandparents.

Then I want you to correlate the entire effort and see if anyone is connected to anyone else. See if they connect to anyone here or to anyone in Washington.

Do you understand me," Doug finished and leaned out to the group in front of him?

"I think the only response they dared to give was to say yes," Joe thought as he looked at Doug.

"If he were green, they would call him the Hulk," Joe thought as the entire office replied in unison, "We understand."

"Ok, they are all yours," Doug said quietly with a disarming smile as he turned and walked slowly back to his office.

"Here is the SD chip with the photos. How can I help?

"Well for now go have a cup of coffee and let us get started. Then you two can help trace relationships of the people associated with the owners of the autos," a master sergeant said as he took the chip.

"Sam duplicate the chip and pass it out," Joe heard him say as Lydia and he walked out.

Their driver was still waiting out by the curb.

"That was fast. Did you guys get listened to," the driver asked?

"Yes, we were. How about taking us back to the house? I want to take a shower and clean up. We will want to come back around 11:00.

Do you mind making a Pizza run? We want to buy the security team here their lunch," Joe asked the driver.

"Are you OK with the pizza we can get on the base? I don't think I will be allowed to go off base," the driver said as he looked at Joe.

"Sure, order a dozen pizzas and mix them up from plain cheese to everything," Joe replied.

"Here, I have the money," Lydia said handing the driver a hundred-dollar bill.

"When did you start carrying that kind of money," Joe said in surprise.

"Right after we got rescued, I figure the next time we may not find such a generous couple that will trust us enough to give us two hundred dollars," Lydia said with a smile.

About the time Joe and Lydia got back to their house, Jorge was called by the base commander and informed about the demonstrators at the gate.

"A couple of your people seem to have arrived at the gate about the same time as the demonstrators. Their quick thinking has given us good pictures that may help us identify who these people are and who may be behind it all," the base commander continued.

"Who on my team are you talking about," Jorge inquired.

"A guy named Joe and a good-looking young lady," was the reply.

"Is there anything I can do to help," Jorge inquired?

Jorge was immediately trying to figure who had leaked what information to whom. He also knew his role was in jeopardy.

"Joe is coming back in a couple of hours to help. "If that is OK," the commander continued.

"Good, he and Lydia are the right ones. I will put my whole team at your disposal if we can be of help," Jorge continued.

"I'll let you know but I think my folks have it under control," the commander said as he hung up.

Jorge immediately called Doug.

"Yes, Lydia and Joe came straight to the security office. We have the SD chip from their camera and have started a search to trace the leak, if possible," Doug replied.

"Thanks, and you know I need the source of the information as soon as possible. It's my head on the cutting block," Jorge commented.

"Yeah, I know the situation," Doug replied.

It was Saturday and usually his team did not work on the weekends, but Jorge put in a call to them and asked them to meet at their work center.

"Thanks for coming in. I don't know if you are aware of it yet but there are demonstrators at all our gates. They are demonstrating against our program and us playing gods," Jorge began.

He had ordered in coffee and some snacks and had made sure everyone was comfortable.

"Joe, it seems you and Lydia were the ones that found out about the demonstrators first. Tell us what you saw," Jorge looked over to where Lydia and Joe were sitting.

"Well," Joe began as he put down the small sausage, cheese, and egg biscuit, "There isn't much to tell except that Lydia and I took pictures of all the participants and all the cars. Then we went over to base security and gave them the SD chip from my camera.

They called in all their folks and are currently working on finding out all they can about the demonstrators.

Lydia and I plan to return shortly to help them."

"What do you plan to do," Tom inquired?

"We are going to take our computers over and use the search feature to seek out information about the participants and all their connections. It is going to be critical to find out who leaked the information," Joe replied

"We can all do that. We can do this as a team, and we can do it from here as well as at the security office. Why don't the two of you act as our representatives and give us the names you want traced," Linda suggested.

"That is a great idea," Jacqueline chimed in.

This was a rare weekend where she had decided to stay in San Antonio versus going home.

"OK, let's plan on it and thank you," Jorge replied.

"We can pull in more of the Door team if it will help," Lydia spoke up as she thought about Darian, Samantha, and R cubed.

"That's another good idea," Aaron spoke up.

"Hey, I just think that we need speed, and more minds will give us that," he reacted when everyone looked at him.

I know of several facial recognition routines that may be of use.

Aaron spoke up so seldom that when he did everyone paid attention.

"You all get organized here. Lydia and I are going to the security office. We ordered in pizza for everyone there," Joe said with a grin as he led the way out of the work center.

"Those two seem to have become the best of friends," Linda said as she put her hand on Tom's and smiled at him.

"Well, I hope they become as good of friends as we are," Tom said as his face again turned red.

"I don't know what those two are talking about, but Tom just turned red," Jacqueline said to Aaron and Jorge.

"Well, they are the only ones I know that have as good a relationship as I do," Jorge said as he looked down at his phone and dialed R cubed.

The driver had all the pizzas in the van when he picked up Lydia and Joe.

"The base pizza shop thanks you," the driver said as he gave Lydia her change.

"For an order this, large they threw in drinks and bread sticks for another five bucks. I hope that was OK," the driver continued.

"That's great, we forgot about the drink part," Lydia replied as she put the change in her purse.

Lydia and Joe each carried in six pizzas and the driver carried the drinks and bread sticks.

"Anyone interested in pizza for lunch," Lydia said as she announced their arrival?

"You bet," was the general reply as everyone looked up from their computers.

"Where should we put them," Joe asked?

"Let's put them in the conference room," the office manager said.

Joe and Lydia set up their laptops at one end of the conference room while everyone gathered around for pizza.

"Thanks, we were just getting ready to break for lunch. Your timing is perfect," Doug said as he walked into the room.

"I talked with the General and told him the two of you are planning to help," Doug spoke between bites of his cheese and sausage pizza.

"Well, it is even better than that. We are only the front for our whole team plus a couple of others. We intend to do a complete trace back today if possible.

Do you guys have any special connections for this search," Joe inquired?

"Yes, we have a couple of databases that should help," Doug said with a smile.

"Your team can have access during this effort but that will end immediately after we are done," Doug continued.

"Let's begin with the end in mind," Lydia commented as Joe, and she sat down and connected with the team back in the work center.

"What do you have in mind," Aaron asked quietly?

"Well, there are only a few sources for this leaked information.

The people on this end involved in our program.

The people associated with the Doorship assembly.

And the people around the President.

We need to work backward from these sources and see if there is any intersection with the states or the people on the license plates.

"Joe and I suspect those around the President," Lydia continued.

"OK, Tom, Linda and I will check out the people associated with the Doorships," Jorge replied.

"Jacqueline, will you Aaron and Darian please run checks with everyone on the base. Begin with all the new support that has been added," Jorge continued to assign tasks.

"Samantha and R cubed please team up with Lydia and Joe and research the political path," Jorge finished.

He wanted the least political people researching the political side. He figured he could protect the least political from the wrath that might follow if that path produced the leak.

"Oh, and I want these files segregated and isolated. When we are done, I plan to eliminate all the information we find," Jorge informed everyone.

"Let's find out where each cabinet member is from," Joe said as he finished his pizza.

"Well, please give me a list of their names," R cube replied.

He had no clue about who was on the President's cabinet.

"What exactly do they do," he wondered out loud?

"Good question," Samantha added.

"Who are the people in the Cabinet," flashed through Lydia's mind as well?

"Once we have their names let's begin with those from the South or those who are opposing party members.

"Why would she have opposing party member in her cabinet," Samantha asked?

A few hours later, Joe let out a whoop.

"I think I have the leak. He is a party member, but he is from Mississippi. His name is Mathew Pinkerton III. He and the President often clash.

He is the nephew of a past clan leader, and he is the great uncle of the owner of one of the cars that I took a picture of," Joe announced.

"This is great news," Jorge replied when Samantha let him know about Joe's find.

After calling Joe and learning more about the connection, Jorge was ready to make the call he knew he needed to make.

"Pardon my call on a Saturday but this is critical," Jorge began as the President's phone was answered by one of the staff.

"The President is busy at the moment. "May I take a message," the staff member asked politely.

"Please let her know that General Martinez called and has some critical information that is extremely time sensitive," Jorge replied.

He figured no one got a direct connection to the President.

"Joe, put your information on an encrypted file and give it to Commander Hardy. Let him handle this from here on," Jorge instructed on his next call.

He then called Doug and gave him instructions.

"Commander, I want you to write up a report and send it to me. This will be for the President's eyes only and I will personally deliver it to her. I need this today. I will be flying out in the morning," Jorge instructed.

Chapter 17: The Cabinet Member

*L*acy as always was thinking about history. She thought about how Julius Cesar learned the hard way about backstabbing friends. At that time, politics literally was a deadly game.

She realized that enemies were not always immediately deadly but almost always were trying to get into a position where their deadliness could be safely executed. She thought that they were seldom brave. She thought of them as devious, deceitful, and cunning but that they should not be underrated.

Lacy MacAdam was not the first president to have enemies trying to take direct action against them.

Some of the stiffest competition came from her presidential contender Mathew Pinkerton III. She remembered the quote from *Machiavelli* in *"The Prince"*, "Keep your friends close and your enemies even closer."

She offered a close friend, Craig Lyjak, the role of Secretary of State. And she offered Mathew the role of Secretary of Defense.

Both had accepted.

This gave her eyes on the enemy and a friend to help. It also gave her an even balance in the Senate.

Mathew's acceptance was good for her administration. He was seen as a hawk, and she was seen as a dove.

The political scene relaxed and moved away from its combative dialogue.

The Presidential contest had been a mean and nasty battle. Starting in Iowa and continuing through every primary contest the tone had been mean and disparaging. Both parties had bitter rivalries through the entire primary season.

Lacy was a veteran politician who served in both the House and the Senate. No newcomer to the political ring, she ran her campaign in a strategically sound and effective manner. She kept to the facts, stayed on message, and stayed away from personal attacks on her competitors.

She consistently asked the electorate for their votes to enable her to deliver a better country for all of them.

One by one the primary campaign competitors dropped away until only Mathew Pinkerton III remained in the contest. Lacy had a narrow lead coming into the convention. Mathew came into the convention convinced he would manipulate the party faithful to put him up as their nominee.

The Democrats at the convention overwhelmingly nominated Lacy Amy MacAdam.

Mathew suffered an embarrassing defeat. To say Mathew was bitter would have been an understatement. He refused to support Lacy during the election and publicly came out against her and her running mate.

The election was bitterly fought at the primaries leading up to the main event. Lacy's ability to weave together and unite a variety of groups with differing views led to an unexpected lopsided victory.

Her coat tails were long enough to give her a Senate where she was one vote shy of the majority and a congress where she had a majority.

She went into office with high hopes and expectations. She soon found out who her true Senate and Congressional friends really were.

She had enough of them to be effective but not enough to deliver the ambitious agenda she had developed for herself and her party.

She rapidly got her key projects underway. One of these projects was her goal to open up the solar system. She wanted new space exploration to once again be the dream of the nation. She knew she needed a lot of luck and a technical breakthrough.

She had asked her scientific advisor and her Chief of Staff to guide her to the formation of a team to deliver her program. Two names had come to the forefront: one for the development of new space going vessels and one for the development of a breakthrough technology.

One was a Marine General who had come up through the aviation part of the Marine Corps. He had demonstrated a keen capability in the improvement of the design of the aircraft he flew.

The other was an Army General who had served in a variety of special assignments and always figured out how to deliver the impossible. He was not seen as a general to command wars but one to guide and develop the out of the box efforts.

The recommendations were in her pocket but non-the-less she was diligent and interviewed a list of over a dozen other potential candidates. Her interviews with the two recommended candidates were not significantly different than any of the others. The one difference in both cases was what Lacy called her "gut feel."

It was what her husband called her intuition.

"Go with your gut," he had told her on the day she was to make her decision.

She did exactly that. Both had proven to be good choices.

General Martinez had delivered the technology, but he had also been in charge during a serious security breach. She had again gone with her gut and had left him in command of the project.

Now there was a new and significant disruption, and he was on his way to see her. He had insisted on a face-to-face, secret meeting.

This insistence caused her concern.

"What in the world would make him ask for a secret meeting," Lacy thought with apprehension.

It was Sunday just before noon when Jorge landed at Ronald Reagan International Airport.

He was dressed in full dress uniform. His plane taxied to the end of the runway and then to one of the hangers managed by some obscure government agency. As he walked down the steps, he was greeted by an agent in a black suit and led to a black limousine.

It was one of the President's limos.

"Men in black, black limousine, what movie did this come from," Jorge thought to himself?

"Well, Lacy got the message about my arrival. She has taken my message seriously enough to send a limo for me," Jorge thought as he sat down in the back seat.

He was not looking forward to this meeting.

"My instructions are to take you to the White House and make sure you are escorted in for a private meeting," the driver informed Jorge.

"I will do as instructed," Jorge replied.

It was clear that his wish to have this visit as invisible as possible was being followed.

This was not a meeting he really wanted to have but he knew no other way to share the news in a secure way.

The ride to the White House took about forty-five minutes. This gave Jorge time to review what he had learned.

He knew that the President would want to be absolutely sure about the source of the leak.

Before coming, Jorge had also made sure that the razor wire security fence on the base could not be seen from the air space outside the base nor from any external vantage point. This was an important point since the razor wire on the placards being shown by the demonstrators outside the gate was a key in pointing to where the leak originated.

The picture with the razor wire had only been shared with the President.

Jorge knew she was not the leak.

"Let's have lunch and then we can discuss the information that you have about this leak. This is just what I was trying to avoid," President Lacy said when she met Jorge in the foyer of the White House.

They walked together to the dining room. As always, her security personnel were with them but stood a discrete distance away.

After lunch Lacy proceeded into her office. She asked her security personnel to exit.

"Now let's hear what you have uncovered about the leak," the President said as she turned to Jorge.

"All information points to Mathew Pinkerton III," Jorge said quietly.

"Are you certain about this," Lacy replied?

Mathew would be one of the worst adversaries to enrage but even worse it would be an illegal act on his part and legal action would be warranted. She would need to take drastic countermeasures to get out of this situation.

"I am going to need concrete evidence to support any action I might take. This is like baiting a bull when you are in the middle of the field with him," Lacy continued.

"The information hunters are going to need specific internet information that ties the leak to Pinkerton. Do you have that kind of connection, and can you do it legally," Jorge inquired?

"I have the means to provide you with internet and phone information and I have the official mechanism to get to that information legally. However, this will affect the country and it will agitate the entire party once it becomes public. I need cover for this operation," was Lacy's next statement.

"Perhaps there is some personal information about his health, or his family. He is seventy-three and there may be something personal he is trying to achieve. If it is anything but a religious belief, perhaps that desired goal can be satisfied in trade for his resignation," Jorge suggested.

"I will take that advice and consider what to do. I will contact the group that will get the connections so you can do the digging," the President replied.

"If you leave now, you will be able to have dinner in the comfort of your home," the President continued as she walked Jorge to the door.

The President spent the next thirty minutes making calls to two members of her "information team" at the NSA.

She gave them the key information she desired and on whom.

It was to be for her eyes only and delivered by hand personally.

Jorge made a call of his own to Joe.

"Dig some more but don't be seen," was all he told Joe.

"I think Jorge wants me to find the back door and some dirt," Joe commented to Lydia.

"Do we know Mathew's IP addresses or where can we get them," Lydia inquired?

"I don't think we have any associated with Pinkerton but let me ask one of the guys in the commander's unit. He was telling me that he knew someone who could get anyone's IP," Joe replied.

Joe made the call and made sure that the information needed to be more than top secret and untraceable.

Two hours later someone rang the doorbell. Darian opened the door only to find an envelope with the name Joe on it.

He looked at the guard and asked who had delivered the envelope.

"There were some kids a few moments ago but they ran through playing tag. There was no one else," the guard replied.

"Joe, are you expecting a message," Darian inquired as he entered the family room with the envelope in hand?

"No, let me see what you have," Joe said as he took the envelope and took out a white sheet of paper with a list of IP addresses.

Lydia did you download the IP address search AP you were talking about," Joe asked as he looked over to where Lydia was on her computer?

"Yes, let's give it a try and see where Mr. Mathew Pinkerton III has been visiting," Lydia said as she began typing in the first IP Address.

They all groaned when the first IP went out to what seemed to be millions of sites.

"Let's save each result in a file. We can pass this on to Jorge for him to give to the appropriate person or agency. This IP seems to be some political information distribution list. Let's just run the rest and then attack the shortest lists on the assumption that the shorter ones may be personal," Lydia suggested.

"Sounds logical to me," Joe replied.

Joe sent a text to Jorge, "Come by for a beer."

Jorge's airplane was just landing when the text came in.

"Sounds good to me, be there in about thirty," Jorge texted back.

"I didn't realize Jorge was so close to getting back. Give me some of those IP's and we can double team this," Joe commented to Lydia as he realized he had nothing to give to Jorge.

"Let's all dig in," Darian said as he and Sam turned on their computers.

"Hey, I have a short IP connection list here. Let's dissect this one and see what we have," Joe spoke up after a long silence amongst the three.

It was only moments later that Lydia gasped and called out, "Oh, my come see this connection. It is to a porn site. I just ran a search of how many times this connection has been made and it is in the hundreds," She announced.

"Well, it may be shocking to think about an old man visiting the site, but it is not illegal," Samantha commented as she looked over Lydia's shoulders.

"Besides, they aren't too bad looking," Joe commented and earned a punch in the shoulder from Lydia.

"This connection is the one that will do him in," Darian commented as he pulled up a kiddie porn site.

Just then the doorbell rang.

"I'll get it," Joe said as he walked down to the kitchen.

The interior guard was sitting at the kitchen table.

"I believe the General is here," Joe commented to the guard as he took out a cold beer and went to the front door.

He wanted to give the guard a chance to be at his best.

"Come in," Joe said as he handed Jorge the beer.

"Have you got something for me," Jorge inquired as he took a short sip?

Joe guided Jorge into the kitchen and presented the guard who stood up and gave a sharp salute.

The sergeant is doing a great job at guarding and protecting us. I thought you should meet him. Joe was stalling to give the team upstairs a chance to finish their digging.

Jorge looked at Joe, smiled and shook his finger and then pointed upstairs.

"Let's go see what the team has dug up," Jorge said as he turned and led the way out of the kitchen.

Joe looked back at the sergeant and gave him a thumbs up.

"Yes, let's go upstairs to our family room. Darian, Samantha, and Lydia have been helping me. In fact, it was Lydia's idea about how to hunt for and find what we found," Joe shared as they walked into the family room.

"Hey, you didn't get us one," Darian said to Joe after shaking Jorge's hand.

"There is one for you in the frig," Joe commented as he went to the small refrigerator and took out four more after looking to Lydia and Samantha for a yes nod.

"We just made two discoveries and there may be more. I think we have uncovered enough that we should turn it over to the commander," Joe continued.

A few moments later, after Lydia had toured Jorge through the find.

Jorge turned to the four and declared, "You are done. Put what you have on a new, un-used memory stick. Give me the memory stick. Take your computers to the commander and tell him I want these computers shredded and returned to me in a bag. You can all get new ones tomorrow. I want you to never say a word to anyone about what you found," Jorge said as he walked over to the small refrigerator and took out another beer.

"You have until I finish this beer," he said as he sat down at the table and dialed what was becoming a familiar number.

President Lacy answered the phone personally.

"I am beginning to recognize your number. I am not sure that this is good," she commented.

"I was thinking the same. I have the locations to dig and would like to send the information directly to the digging team. Please send my Commander that information. I am back and planning to have dinner," Jorge said slowly and hoped Lacy understood his request.

"You do that and thank you for coming to see me," President Lacy closed and hung up.

She immediately made a call that would provide the information General Martinez wanted.

"He was very cryptic. This probably means he has some damaging information and wants to get it into my hands without involving me directly or linking it back to his team. I am glad that I followed my instincts and did not fire him," Lacy thought to herself.

Jorge took another sip of his beer and dialed the Commander.

"Doug, you will get a cryptic piece of unknown information. It is for me. Please print it and then erase the message from your computer. Joe will be bringing over four computers that I want shredded. Shred them, put the pieces in a bag and send me the bag. Don't ask and I won't have to make up any stories," Jorge concluded.

"I understand. Welcome back. I hope you have a good dinner," Doug replied.

He knew better than try to make sense of what was transpiring. He trusted Jorge to keep him in the clear.

Jorge turned to announce he had finished his beer only to find Lydia, Joe, Samantha, and Darian standing with a memory stick held out to him.

"Thank you. I enjoyed the beer. Dinner at home is waiting. You all have a great evening after you drop off those computers to the commander," Jorge said with a smile and nod.

He left by after telling them all "Thank You."

"This has been a good day for the Door program," Jorge thought to himself as he walked out.

On Monday, the President requested a meeting for Tuesday afternoon with Mathew Pinkerton III. The purpose of the meeting was to agree on the next steps in Mr. Pinkerton's handling of some sensitive affairs in the Middle East.

"How urgent is this meeting? His calendar is full at the moment," Mr. Pinkerton's support secretary inquired.

"The President said it was of the highest priority," the President's appointment secretary said truthfully.

Meanwhile the Justice Department was discretely engaged at the highest level to determine if the computers utilized in Mr. Pinkerton's office and home could be seized based on suspected child pornography.

By Tuesday afternoon the President had all the information she needed to know that Mathew Pinkerton had indeed leaked the location and main purpose of the Door program. She technically had him endangering the good of the country. She could prosecute him as a traitor that had leaked information damaging to the country.

However, such an approach would damage her party as well as the country.

Mathew Pinkerton was escorted into a small private office with a table and a large flat screen. The only other person in the room was the President.

Mathew knew that something was up, but he thought he had the issue covered.

"Matt, you have betrayed my trust in you. You have the choice to resign and get out of politics or information that will destroy both you and your family will be leaked to the press. Before you say one word, let me show you some footage that will help you understand the situation," Lacy said as the door to the room closed.

Lacy pressed play on the computer screen and the video played.

The first part showed the picture of Mathew's great nephew managing the demonstrators outside of the gate.

"This came about because you arranged for it to happen. Don't say a word because what comes next will make it clear what will happen if you don't cooperate," Lacy commented.

The next part showed an IP number and then the kiddy porn site.

"This is the IP from your computer. What you are doing is inappropriate and illegal. This will inadvertently be leaked just as you leaked key government information. No one will know who leaked it.

You cook up whatever story you wish to tell but by Friday I want your resignation and I want you to walk away from all party activities.

You will appoint your deputy director as the acting Secretary of Defense.

There will be no second chance. Do I make myself clear and do you accept?" the President said as she slammed her hand on the table.

Lacy could see the anger and hatred in Mathew's eyes. His face was now an almost white color. This appearance was from a man that went regularly to the tanning booth.

Lacy held his gaze until he finally broke and looked down.

"This is a cheap trick. I personally think you are the wrong person for your job, and I think you are a danger to the country. I also know you will do as you say. Yes, you have my resignation, but I will use all the means I have to get back at you," Mathew said in a barely controlled manner.

His face was now red, and he was shaking with anger.

"How dare this bitch do this to me," was on the forefront of his mind?

He was close to personally attacking her. He was shaking uncontrollably.

Lacy pressed the button to summon the escorts that would take Mathew out.

It was clear to her that Mathew was not going to go peacefully away. She would need to act immediately to minimize the damage to the party and the risk to the Door program.

Once Mathew was escorted out of the meeting room, she went to her office and put in a call to the FBI and the Department of Justice and told them to proceed with the immediate confiscation of all the computers in Mathew's office and home.

They were to validate that the links to the kiddie porn sites existed and determine if there was any other damaging information.

They were to wait exactly one month before charging him with every valid charge that could be brought.

Chapter 18: Mathew Pinkerton III

ℋatred is poison to the soul. Subsequently, haters have small souls. Those with small souls care little about the people around them or people that may suffer due to action on their part.

Haters have differing degrees of precision. There are laser haters that can focus their hate on a single person. There are intermediate haters that hate programs or general customs. Finally, there are the shotgun haters who blast away at any hate direction that captures their attention at the moment.

Mathew Pinkerton III thought of himself as a laser hater but in reality he was a shotgun hater. He wanted his target to be at the center of his aim, but he was also randomly blasting away all around his target. Hurt her, hurt anyone that might help her…hell hurt all those bastards that refused to support me.

"I am going to destroy the bitch," Mathew thought to himself as he was escorted out of the White House.

His personal car and driver were waiting for him.

"Take me to the office," Mathew instructed as he got into the back seat.

He wanted to clear his computer of all its connections. He wished he were more computer literate so he could do it himself, but he had several aids he could count on to do it for him.

He had a rude awakening on the return to his office.

"What do you mean all our computers were confiscated," he shouted at his office staff?

"The justice department officials, escorted by the police removed all our computers less than fifteen minutes ago," a teary-eyed secretary informed him.

"The bitch moved faster than I thought she would," Mathew thought to himself as he slammed the door to his office.

He knew he needed to go home and destroy his family's personal computers.

His phone rang.

"Mathew a group of men led by the FBI and some Department of Justice officials just took all our computers and they are searching the house. I tried to stop them, but they gave me official looking papers authorizing them to do this," his wife said.

Mathew sat down. His father had told him to never underestimate an enemy.

"I just underestimated my worst enemy," he thought to himself.

"How had she done it?"

The only people who could have given her this intel had to be the people associated with the Door program.

"That son of a bitch General Martinez and his crew somehow traced the leak to me," Mathew continued his thoughts.

"I am screwed but by god, I am going to screw that entire lot," he continued his musing.

He immediately thought through the details of his three plans. He still needed to complete plans B and C.

He realized that he was running out of time.

His arrest a few weeks later and the grand jury hearing were damming. Only his longtime political connections kept him from being charged with treason.

He began taking a higher level of risk but hell he was already screwed.

He was under the equivalent of house arrest from the very first day. His trial date was set. Mathew knew he was facing jail time. His only hope was to get sentenced to a low security level prison.

Mathew purchased a new phone to make a few key calls. Once he had made these calls, he destroyed the phone by pulverizing it with a sledgehammer. The remains were nothing but sand like crystals. He hoped this would erase all the information he had exposed during the call. In this day and age of technology it was hard to tell where stuff ended up.

The calls had gone out to two people he knew hated the President as much as he did. One was his grandniece and the other an old friend in the construction business.

He made a third call to a person who had been an adversary. The information going to that person would be sent via a human information transporter. It would cost him a significant sum of money but at this point Mathew was not concerned about his finances.

The family trust would take care of his wife and the government would most likely be taking care of him.

Mathew had decided that he would bring an end to the Door program before it had a chance to begin.

His three plans were in motion, and they would most certainly take the program out.

"Let's see how she and that ass, General Martinez and his crew of puppets like these apples," Mathew thought as he imagined and played through each of the three scenarios.

Once again, he played his father's saying, "Always have plans A, B and C. Make sure one of them works,"

His father had been a Bourbon Democrat and a leader in the White Cap movement in Mississippi.

Mathew had been influenced by his participation in the many meetings and family outings he had attended as a young boy. His intellect had made it clear in his mind that most of the philosophy that was pushed as gospel was biased and slanted to satisfy the need to feel superior by its white followers.

He, however, saw it as an opportunity to gain influence and power both in his daily life and later in his political endeavors.

"It has worked all my life," Mathew thought as he continued his musing.

Rather than face trial and go through a long embarrassing experience and face the humiliation of having the more sordid material from the web site connections being made public, Mathew pleaded guilty to leaking sensitive government information.

His lawyers were able to negotiate a twenty-year sentence in a low security prison.

"I am going to use this place to run my campaign against the bitch," Mathew concluded as he thought about the disruption and embarrassment he and his family had suffered. The worst embarrassment had been averted but none-the-less the fires of Mathew's hatred were stoked and now burned with new intensity.

His grand-niece, Madeline came to see him and together they discussed ways to attack the President and to sabotage the Door program.

"I have a contact that is involved in the programing of the environmental control system for the spaceships they plan to launch," Madeline volunteered as they walked the grounds of the prison.

She had been looking for a purpose in life and this gave her the challenge she had been looking for.

"I will work with Victor to set up the alternate means of destroying the Door effort," she volunteered as they discussed the potential of blowing the ship up.

"I have made contact with a group in the Middle East. They are willing to launch a missile to destroy the launch rocket. All they will need is to know where the first launch will be," Mathew continued to share the details with Madeline.

"How do I get that information to your contact," Madeline inquired.

"This is old fashioned, but it keeps us off the monitored electronic systems. Place an ad in the New York Times for a Middle Eastern house cleaner. In the ad put the map coordinates of the launch location. My contact will know what to do," Mathew replied.

"Thanks for the help," Mathew said as he gave Madeline a departing hug.

"I feel a little guilty, but she seems to relish this activity," Mathew thought as he waved as she got into her car.

Madeline left that first meeting with new purpose and energy. She had been drifting along wondering about her purpose in life. Taking action against the woman she despised seemed like the perfect scenario.

"I am going to make it my goal to see that she gets defeated in her next election," Madeline thought as she drove away from the prison.

Madeline looked too much like her grand uncle to be considered good looking, in the fashion runway sense of the word, but she knew she was considered classy. She was slender, had her hair styled to frame her face and wore the latest fashion. She also mixed with the top of society in and around Miami.

An observer would have thought her to be a successful, happy professional.

Her connection with a programmer for NASA enabled her to get a back door put into the spaceship environmental control system. The person who provided the back door was not aware of its purpose.

Madeline had convinced him she was working for another defense contractor and their interest was supported by the Door program. He thought it was for additional monitoring.

Madeline had earned her degree in computer programing and was more than capable of programing the shut-down routine on her own.

She disguised it as an environmental monitoring program. She provided detailed written descriptions for each of the modules in her program. It was truly a monitoring program. Most people examining it would most likely read the written explanation and just glance at the code.

In the monitoring code was a one-line, time-based replication routine that when activated would constantly replicate itself and cause the environmental control system to shut down when the computer was overloaded.

She sent this "monitoring" program back to the person that had provided the back door and it was automatically linked in with the rest of the code.

During this same time, she followed the news and was able to determine where the first launch was to be. She was not fooled by the Door program manager's attempt to hide the first launch site.

Through another connection in NASA, she monitored the location of General Martinez. When the General traveled to Brazil, she concluded the first launch would be from that location.

"I hope the folks Uncle Mathew mentioned read the paper every day," Madeline thought as she placed the ad for the Middle Eastern cleaning lady and put in the coordinates and date of the first launch site.

Her connection with Uncle Mathew's old friend had happened in the week following her visit to the prison.

Victor Montique owned a global construction company.

His company had the contract to provide the soil to be used in the Door reconstitution process. There was a specific quality and cleanliness specification that the soil needed to meet.

Everything that went on the Doorship was thoroughly checked. However, Victor knew that the soil was no longer being checked. The paperwork was always reviewed and recorded. The checking had stopped almost immediately after the fiftieth truck load. There were just too many other items that needed checking and dirt did not make that list.

"I will handle the preparation of the material," Victor had informed Madeline when they discussed the plan.

Victor's wealth and current influence had been the result of his long-time connection with Mathew. He credited Mathew with having given him the means to rise to his current level of influence.

Victor was a close confidant and had worked on all of Mathew's political campaigns.

"I'm not too keen on doing this but I owe him," Victor thought to himself as he made contact with the connection in Kenya.

His other connection on the placing of the material on the door-ship was straight forward. The person involved had no clue that giving the soil placement location was anything other than a procedural requirement.

Victor would put the explosive material in place, but he would not directly pull the trigger. He purposely refused to think about the lives that would be lost by his actions.

He was not only a follower, but he was a conveniently a heartless one.

Chapter 19: Plans for the Launch

Lacy understood that people observed the action of leaders. This observation organically got translated into the attitude and behavior of the observer. She felt that the impact of a leader's actions was magnified many fold when it was natural, consistent, and personal.

Lacy MacAdam understood the power of direct involvement. It was a natural attribute of her character. Her interest in the Door program was personal. She wished she could be one of the volunteer Doormen or in her case Doorwoman.

This was truly a personal passion, and she was happy to be in the position to see the solar system opened during her watch.

She marveled at the accomplishments of the brilliant scientists like Tom and Linda Hughes who somehow had figured out how to transmit and reconstitute living matter. To reconstitute a human mind was something out of science fiction.

She smiled as the phrase, "mind blowing," flashed through her mind.

If she could, she would gladly be on the Door team.

The Door team followed the political fallout with interest.

Mathew Pinkerton III was indicted for his National Security breach. During the investigation that followed he was exposed in the media as a pedophile.

President MacAdam held a press conference to announce her surprise and disappointment.

"I want the country to remember the great contributions made by Mathew to his party and to his country. This morning I accepted his resignation from the cabinet. It is hard for me to accept the allegations. The Justice Department will appropriately follow the required review process.

I will rely on our system of justice to take the appropriate actions based on the evidence provided," the President closed her announcement.

She had artfully nullified one of her greatest opponents.

The evidence that had been gathered was damming and ironclad.

Lacy refused any further discussion on the topic of Mathew and within a few days he was no longer in the news.

She personally traveled to San Antonio on a surprise visit to thank Jorge and the Door team.

Jorge called together his core team for a meeting with President MacAdam.

"Team our President has taken the time to visit us personally. I will let her do the talking," Jorge said in introduction.

"I believe you all know how close I came to firing Jorge when Joe, Lydia and Darian were kidnapped. He presented himself with confidence and I went with my gut feel. That gut feel has served me well in the past and it certainly did this time.

Jorge has made me aware of the role this team played but especially Joe and Lydia. It seems Joe and his partners, Lydia, Darian, and Samantha have their toes in all the adventures this team has.

I came to personally thank all of you.

I also came to let you know how important this program is to the world.

The full weight and power of the US government is behind its success. I have personally called in all my favors to see that it gets launched and out to space.

Your efforts in the next few months are critical. I have made this clear to the General.

"Go and come back victorious or on your shield," Lacy said with a smile.

She then went around the room personally thanking each person and shaking hands.

"Joe, you seem the unlikely hero, but you keep turning up. I am so glad that this transmission technology had the side effect of curing your cancer.

"Thank you," Lacy said giving Joe a hug.

"Lydia your insight on how to connect Mr. Pinkerton to his vices, proved to be invaluable.

"And Darian, I understand you have made good progress from being a lady's man to being one of the top Door Men.

This is said to be especially true by Samantha," Lacy closed with a chuckle.

She then looked around and thanked whoever had leaked the pedophile information to the media. She smiled and added that she was sure it was no one on the Door team.

This level of detailed knowledge did not go unnoticed by the Door team or Jorge.

"Thank you all. I need to catch my ride back to my Washington political treadmill. Give me the Door to our Solar System," Stacy said in closing as she walked out and pumped her fist up and down in emphasis.

"That was really nice of her to come all this way to personally thank us," Lydia said after the President left the room.

Lydia knew that she would never admit to having leaked the information.

"Well, if we can all meet our timeline commitments, we will deliver her a ready to go system this coming year.

We are on track with our three transports.

China has said their system will be ready. Brazil and Mexico have offered us launch capacity. Japan has just come through with another spaceship and launch capacity. This puts us in great shape.

The bottleneck is the production of the Transport units," Ryan rattled off the project status.

A few moments later the "senior members" of the team; Jorge, Tom, Linda, Jacqueline, and Aaron, as the younger members called them, returned from seeing the President off.

"Team, I am honored to lead this effort.

Your capability and actions will make us successful.

You have saved my career and the President's. If we deliver the Door program this coming year during the summer and early fall, we will deliver a second term for her.

As you know her actions have riled her party and she needs the extra leverage to overcome the internal strife as well as to give her a shield from the opposing party," Jorge said as he looked around at his core team.

"I think everybody has their work cut out for them. We will have our regular leadership meeting tomorrow morning. At that time, we will give our updates and evaluate our progress. Let's all get to work," Jorge announced as he looked around to everyone.

"Let's go see General Delaney and his team about the construction of the Doorships," Joe said as he, Darian and Lydia walk out to their car.

They had obtained one to drive around the base so they would not have to have a driver always waiting.

They could not get off base other than when they flew to Houston where the Delaney team had their headquarters. Once done working with the Delaney team, the three always made it a point to go out briefly in Houston before returning.

They had adopted the practice of inviting some of the other members of the Door team to come with them.

Samantha, R cubed, and Yara had become regular partakers of this offer. Yara was a new team member from Brazil. She and R cubed seemed to have hit it off. It looked like Samantha and Darian had something going.

Joe and Lydia kept quiet about all of this, but they were pleased that these relationships were taking shape. They knew they had each other and that was more than enough for them. Their brush with death and the miracle of the transport-receive process had a big effect on their attitude and thinking.

"Well, we have our work cut out," Joe said as he looked over the plans on how the Doorship was to be assembled in space.

"I like the fact that all the joints lock together in an airtight fit. I would prefer that we also weld every exterior joint for additional structural integrity," R cubed spoke up when he reviewed the assembly instructions.

"That would take almost a year to accomplish," one of the design team commented.

"Yes, it would but that is not an issue if we have it done via a welding robot. It could be doing the job as we traverse the solar system. We just need to make sure we have a welding robot," R cubed quietly fired back.

R cubed got agreement to the robot welder later from Jerry.

"I will lay out an assembly practice process. We will first practice the assembly on dry land. Then if we feel it is necessary, we will simulate the assembly underwater," Samantha shared with the team.

"We will need to be ready by Thanksgiving. We will practice until the week before Christmas.

The General has scheduled all of us for two weeks off over Christmas.

Launch of all the components will commence the first of February.

Our team members will go up by the first of March to begin assembly. The assembly will take place over the summer months.

Finally, on Labor Day we will begin our Door delivery journey," Joe rattled off the timeline.

Joe and Lydia had become the leaders of the Door Delivery Team or DDT as they began to call themselves.

Joe was primarily focused on the Doorship assembly.

Lydia was focused on getting the transmit-receive (TR) units ready. She, Linda, and Tom worked closely with a production team in the Development Corporation (C4ISR) division.

She was often away with the two in Los Angeles at the production facility.

There Linda and Tom tested every unit at least one hundred times. Tom used exactly one hundred mice. These mice were in turn being tested and monitored by Jacqueline and Aaron.

The final test was always with a two-hundred-and-fifty-pound pig. These pigs would join the first two for long term observation.

Lydia escorted every unit back to Lakland airbase where they were stored under guard by Commander Hardesty's security force. She personally tagged each unit in a key spot and only she knew where and what the tag was.

This was something she and Joe had talked about doing.

"Mark them so you will know if someone has broken into the unit. I don't want to know how you do it. It will be only you who knows about this precaution," Joe had suggested to her.

Lydia though about this for a long time and then came up with a simple way to know if someone had opened the container the units were in or if someone had opened the doors to either unit.

She carried her marking equipment in her purse.

The transmit-receive unit for a ship was a ten-foot high, three-foot diameter ceramic tube. The transmission disassembly ring mounted on a single rod ran up the outside of the tube. The resulting energy burst was guided magnetically out the top while it was aimed at the target receiver. The energy burst could be guided to the on-board receiver and utilized to create the transmitted object.

These units could be used locally by routing the transmit signal to the onboard receiver. In this way the unit could be used to extend the lives of the Doormen.

The material for re-constitution was stored in several ceramic containers.

The amount of material for the onboard systems would be enough for three transmissions per Doorman.

A material gathering system, designed to gather material in space would be deployed once the Doorship was in space. This would be used to re-fill the receiver material hoppers with the material found in space.

The units to be dropped off near each planet were part of a structure that could be anchored to one of the moons of the planets. They were also designed to be freely located in space and just orbit the selected planet.

The Moon and Mars would each have a unit on the surface. These two units would immediately go into use.

These units had the reconstitution material for twenty people. The first twenty people would then make sure that the units got filled with additional reconstitution material. This would immediately open the Moon and Mars for the arrival of large numbers of scientists and explorers.

The units selected for orbital life had triple the capacity of reconstitution material than those to be landed on planets. This would provide for a minimum of three exploratory missions for each unit.

Several of the planets were scheduled to have two or even three units orbiting them. This was the only way to accomplish the ambitious plans described by the President.

The level of accomplishment and ambition surprised Tom.

"I really like the thinking and the scope that has been proposed.

President MacAdam really has pushed to get this to be successful. Her vision is expansive and will serve mankind well. I hope history recognizes her contribution," Tom commented to the team during one of their weekly planning meetings.

"I believe her ability to unify this endeavor was a monumental step forward. The fact that you and Linda made the break-through will be what will be remembered by history," Jeffery Yang replied.

He and his team were now fully integrated into the effort and were focused on making it a success. He was impressed with Tom's and Linda's uncanny scientific intuition. He wished he would have had such a pair on his team.

"I like the idea of taking off for Christmas. I also know that a significant number on the team also celebrate the Chinese New Year. Perhaps we can arrange the work so each holiday can be celebrated. I suggest we arrange the workload to accommodate this," Jeffrey suggested.

"I think that proposal is a good one. Let's make sure the team has full capability during both periods.

Ryan, please work on the schedule and arrange it. Let me know if there are any issues," Jorge responded.

He was thinking about the team that would be put into space. This would be their last days for perhaps their lifetime.

"Let's make sure everyone involved lets us know their personal holiday needs. We will make the arrangements necessary for everyone to enjoy their remaining months here on Earth. Soon enough they will be away for what maybe a lifetime," Jorge concluded the meeting.

Chapter 20: The Wedding

There is no doubt that each person potentially has multiple soulmates. There is also no doubt that many of these soul mates never find each other. The precious nature of two people meeting each other and discovering they are not only soul mates but have the capacity to be lifelong friends can be labeled a miracle.

Lydia and Joe were two individuals that first bravely faced their own deaths and then they not only discovered their own inner strength, but they discovered each other. They were one of the lucky ones to find their soul mates.

Their new friends immediately recognized this relationship. Linda had tagged it when Joe had come to the lab to witness Lydia's transmission and reception. She had her own soul mate and was pleased when the therapeutic nature of transmission and reconstitution was discovered allowed Lydia and Joe to have the same experience.

The wedding announcement was no surprise to her. It warmed her heart.

Lydia and Joe had let a small inner circle know about their Christmas plans. They were planning to get married a few days after Christmas at the ranch where Joe had grownup.

All of the inner circle accepted their invitation immediately.

Lydia's parents were overjoyed. Her brother was excited about a Texas ranch wedding.

"Your mother is going to be very happy about this," Joe's father had replied when he was asked to host the wedding at the ranch.

"I knew I had been kept around for something like this. Your mother will so enjoy this," Uncle Ted said in closing the description of the up-coming event.

I didn't know this would be such an important event. I was trying to keep it low key," Lydia had confided to Joe.

They had gone to the ranch for Thanksgiving dinner to make their intention known.

"Oh, my wedding was never going to be any lower key than this. If Uncle Ted were controlling the invite list every person in the county would be on it. You will see Uncle Ted in his element during the wedding preparation and the wedding celebration. He will be in his element.

Now look at my Dad and see how laid back he seems. However, I know him well enough that he is probably periodically throwing in suggestions to Ted and then seeing if they took," Joe replied with a smile. He personally was as happy as he had ever hoped to be.

He watched as Uncle Ted went into full preparation mode.

He ordered a fifty-by-fifty-foot canvas cover to be erected in the flat pasture area next to the house.

He rented and parked a fully equipped RV for each guest family.

The parents of the bride got the best room in the house.

And Lydia's brother got the foreman's room in the ranch's hired hand area.

The food would be the best Uncle Ted could think up.

He also had a twenty-foot high, live blue spruce trucked in. He hired a crew to plant, decorate and light it. It would be there for Christmas and then be the backdrop for the wedding.

He had strategically positioned the spruce to be part of the long-term garden layout.

The celebration was planned for the entire Christmas to New Year time frame. The wedding would be smack in the middle.

The list ended up growing to about fifty people, including a few young children.

"No problem, we will have the facilities for everyone," Ted declared.

Meanwhile Lydia and Joe went shopping for their wedding outfits. They were going to be in matching western range outfits. Each would have a new white Stetson hat.

The evening before they left the Ranch to go back to the base Joe's father pulled out a ring case with two plain gold bands. Each gold band had the same inscription; "I will be with you forever."

"I would be honored if the two of you would use these. I have kept them for this occasion," he said quietly.

Joe knew this was a pivotal moment for the family.

Lydia stood up and went to Trey and gave him a hug. "I am honored to be given the opportunity to continue the family tradition of eternal love."

This was the first time in years that Joe had seen tears run down his father cheeks.

"I knew I loved you the moment I saw you and now I know it is forever," Joe whispered to Lydia as he gave her a hug.

He looked over to see his Dad wipe tears from his eyes as well.

Uncle Ted blew his nose and came over to Lydia and gave her a hug.

"Thank you, I think Mom is happy tonight," Joe said to his Father.

The days between Thanksgiving and the Christmas holidays was a blur.

The demonstrators at the gate had reduced in numbers and now the regulars were there at all times. However, the work on the base was unabated.

The arrangement of getting everyone out for a Friday and Saturday away from the base via the airways worked very well. Flights were arranged to San Diego, LA, and San Francisco on the West Coast. Houston and Dallas were a helo ride away. Special arrangements were made for those desiring to go to other locations. Orlando was a big attraction for those wanting to see Disney World.

Joe and Lydia went to the ranch every Friday night to help with the wedding arrangements.

Uncle Ted had mowed a landing area in the shape of a target.

"I thought this would help the pilots. They all seem to be great young men," Uncle Ted had commented.

He always either had the helicopter pilots in for breakfast or for dinner depending on the timing of the arrival.

Ferrying Joe and Lydia became a prime sought-after assignment for the pilots.

Lydia's family accepted Trey's invitation to spend a vacation on the ranch from December 15 until after the New Year.

"Thank You. This will be a great time for my family," Lydia said as she gave Trey a hug.

Trey and Lydia seemed to have an especially close relationship. They would often go for a walk around the garden, yard, and talk.

"You found a treasure. She is as good looking, probably smarter and as loving as your mother," Uncle Ted commented as Joe, and he sat on the porch watching the two.

"I never told you before, but both your dad and I loved and courted your mother. He and I have been best friends all our lives.

She told us that she loved us both, but she chose your Dad.

I left and went to culinary school during their early marriage years. When I learned she was ill, I returned to be with her and your Dad. When she passed away, your Dad and I became inseparable.

We helped each other through that rough time. Our love for her has never died.

It seems you have found someone very similar to your mother. Lydia is a sweetheart," Uncle Ted said as he dried some tears from his eyes.

"Thank you for letting me know.

Both of you have always kept my mother in the major events of my life. I feel she is always with us. "Thank you," Joe replied as he sipped his coffee and watched Lydia talking with his Dad.

He had been blessed to have been raised by these two wise and practical men.

"And thanks Mom," he finished his thought as he took another sip.

The preparations for the wedding were the primary focus on the ranch. The cattle herding was left to the three capable crew members that lived on the ranch.

Their living area was under a total overhaul, but they could see that after the wedding their living quarters would be totally renovated and new. They were quite willing to be slightly inconvenienced during the Christmas period.

Besides, they knew Uncle Ted would be cooking up a storm and they would benefit by enjoying some of the best food in the world.

Uncle Ted checked every detail to make sure he would have the perfect arrangement.

The number of guests was tallied to be seventy people. Some would only be on the ranch for a couple of days.

Twenty-one people would stay between seven and fourteen days. Ted assigned each person to a specific accommodation depending on their length of stay.

He rented the RV's from a Houston based RV fabricator. He arranged for temporary plumbing with a local plumbing company.

The construction in the crew's quarters occupied at least a dozen local contractors.

The tent for the wedding was erected a week before the event. Ted wanted to make sure it was in place and that there would be no issues with its assembly.

"Don't forget to arrange for someone to conduct the wedding ceremony," Trey commented one evening.

He knew by the look on Ted's face that he had forgotten that detail.

The Mayor was one of the friends they had invited. This made it easy to arrange for someone to officiate the ceremony.

Lydia's brother, Jarret arrived a few days earlier than her parents. He was picked up at the Amarillo airport by Uncle Ted. On his first morning he got some horseback riding lessons and then was sent out to work with the rest of the ranch hands minding the cattle.

"You are going to earn your keep here at the ranch," Uncle Ted said in a simulated gruff voice.

Jarret was assigned to one of the bunks where the rest of the ranch hands were sleeping.

"Break him in easy but make sure he knows what it is to be a cowboy," Uncle Ted told the foreman.

"Well, you seem to be getting that cowboy tan line across your forehead," Lydia commented when she saw Jarret a week later.

Joe had two large stallions. One was black and the other white.

"These are Yin and Yang. They are getting along in years now but still have a few more to go. Let's go into town and buy you a saddle. You can ride Yang," Joe said as he took Lydia for a tour of the horse barn.

Both horses had access to the large field that went down toward the river.

Later Joe took Lydia out for a ride down to the River and his favorite swimming hole.

"How about a quick swim," Joe suggested?

"I don't have my swimsuit," Lydia replied.

"I have never used one to swim here," Joe countered with a smile as he tied Yin to a small tree and began to undress.

He ran and jumped into the pool feet first. He knew it was too shallow to dive into.

Lydia hesitated for a moment and then followed Joe's lead.

"She is just gorgeous," Joe thought as he watched Lydia jump in after him.

"You know we have not talked about our honeymoon. I have been thinking a few days in Hawaii would be a great get away. I hear Maui is a great place in the winter," Lydia suggested as they sat drying off after their swim.

"I am game. Let's go home and make our plans," Joe said as he stood up to put on his clothes.

Christmas was a week later. Lydia's parents arrived on the Friday before Christmas.

The rest of the smaller inner Door core team all showed up via various routes on Saturday. Christmas was on a Monday.

The Wedding would be the following Saturday.

The newlyweds would fly out Saturday evening and be in Hawaii by morning. They had arranged for an Ocean View condominium in Waialua.

"I am so happy to have everyone here at the Ranch," Trey announced on their first evening dinner.

The dinner was being served outdoors under the large tent. Trey had hired four waiters and waitresses to serve the drinks.

Uncle Ted had steaks, shrimp and sausages on the grill being attended by a separate cook master. Drinks were available at the bar and then refills would be handled by the waiters and waitresses.

A small four-piece band played Christmas and Old-time favorite music.

"Wow your dad and uncle have gone over the top," Lydia's mother commented to Joe.

"Yes, they told me that they wanted to be heard in heaven," Joe said with a smile.

Lydia now understood this inside joke and smiled at Joe.

The breakfasts, lunches and dinners were made to order. Everyone gathered under the tent and enjoyed themselves and the amazing selection of culinary delights.

Uncle Ted had the Christmas tree planted but it was not yet fully decorated. The top half of the tree was done by a person Ted had hired. This person had to stand on a temporary platform to decorate the top half. The lights had been put on all the way down but there were no decorations on the bottom half.

Only Lydia's immediate family and Joe's family were spending Christmas together.

On Christmas Eve day Uncle Ted had a tree decoration party. The family members were all given a box of decorations and asked to put them on while singing Christmas songs.

"I have never seen Uncle Ted so energized. He really loves having all of these people here," Joe commented to Lydia.

"Yes, and I know your dad seems really happy as well. I am glad we get along so well. He is a jewel," Lydia replied.

She had come to understand Trey's love for his wife and to understand a lot about Joe's solid personality.

Her mother had commented, "You have picked well."

Jarret had taken to ranching and talked about coming out after his high school graduation.

"We'd love to have you over the summer, but I would encourage you to get into some good college and get some more education. Being a cowboy grows old after a couple of years," Trey had commented one evening during the dinner conversation.

"I grew up on the ranch and loved it. However, I was determined to get out of Canadian and see the larger world. I am glad I tried. How else would I have met your sister," Joe added?

Lydia's parents took to both Trey and Uncle Ted. They were surprised to learn that this was the only family Joe had.

Christmas day was spent exchanging small gifts and taking relaxing walks around the grounds.

Sitting and exchanging stories on the porch took up the afternoon. Uncle Ted was in his element, being able to tell his stories to a new set of listeners.

The biggest present went to Jarret.

"This paint is for you. You can keep it here at the ranch and come back to ride any time. If you find a place near where you live, I will have it delivered to you in Tennessee," Uncle Ted said as he handed the reins of the horse to Jarret.

"Wow, I can't believe it. I don't deserve it," Jarret replied.

"Well, I agree about not deserving it, but it really is a beautiful horse," Lydia said as she gave Uncle Ted a hug.

"To go with the horse, you are going to need a saddle," Trey said as he carried out a new dark brown leather saddle.

"There wasn't much left over of our Christmas fund so all we could get for Joe and Lydia was an apple for their horses," Uncle Ted said as he brought out two apples each on the end of an arrow.

"And since Ted wanted to play cupid, we had to buy matching bows and arrows," Trey said as he presented Joe and Lydia with a pair of compound bows.

"These are beautiful," Joe and Lydia said almost in unison.

"I set up a target range about a quarter of a mile north of the barn. All practice will be away from the rest of us," Uncle Ted said as he got a hug from Lydia.

"Well, I am not sure we are going to be able to match Uncle Ted and Trey, but Joe and I got each of you what we thought might be unique," Lydia said as she presented her present first to Uncle Ted.

"We would like you to wear that on the Wedding day. Actually, we want you in the kitchen getting everything ready," Joe commented as Uncle Ted tried on his Chef's outfit.

It had his name embroidered on the shoulder, Master Chef Ted Stratford, and it had a small insignia that was the picture of the ranch house at Sunrise.

"I figured I would have to get my Dad a better outfit for the Wedding, than he normally wears," Joe said as he placed several boxes in front of his father.

The outfit had been made by one of the Canadian seamstresses. She had made some outfits for Trey in the past and still had his size. It was a stylized tuxedo designed to fit over cowboy boots. It had the same insignia that was on Uncle Ted's chef outfit, on the lapel. The final touch was a new black Stetson with a white band.

"I don't know when you had time to arrange this, but this is a beautiful outfit," Trey commented.

"Well, I would like to throw in one more thing from the Tabata family," Jarret said as he presented a box to Trey and one to Uncle Ted.

Both opened the boxes up to find black, spit polished boots that were exactly the same but for the shoe size.

"Thank you all. This is really a happy time here at the ranch," Uncle Ted offered.

For the next few days, all focus was on getting things prepared for the wedding.

Joe and Lydia spent their time developing their skill with the bow and riding to the swimming hole. It had been unseasonably warm but on their last swim the weather had returned to a more normal cold temperature.

"I guess that will be our last swim. We will have to wait for Maui for our next one," Joe commented as he finished getting dressed.

Uncle Ted had a crew that he was supervising in the various aspects of hosting some seventy people.

The van serving as the pick-up bus was in constant circulation.

Most of the team from San Antonio arrived via helicopter.

Jarret had become a tour guide, giving horseback rides to his family and other early guests.

Getting together for meals, relaxing, and talking under the tent, sitting on the ranch veranda allowed the guests to get to know each other much more closely than most other wedding situations.

"This is a good moment for the Door team," Jorge commented.

"Yes, I believe it is. I want to thank Joe and Lydia for including me in the invitation," Jeffrey Yang added.

He, Joe, and Lydia had developed a very good relationship in the weeks since the Door program had been integrated. His three Door candidates had commented about Joe's and Lydia's inclusion and the personal touch they gave to ensure all the new arrivals felt at home.

"Joe and Lydia have become my best friends. I hope that you and I end up having the same relationship those two have," Darian added as he gave Samantha a hug.

The guests had been asked not to bring any gifts but if they desired, they should make a contribution to the Children's Care Society posted on the wedding web page.

On the Wedding Morning, Joe and Lydia took a long ride on Yin and Yang.

"I am going to miss this when we get out in space," Lydia commented.

"I have been thinking about this for some time. Once we get the Doors delivered, we can transmit back to Earth. The ranch will still be here.

I just don't know how much time will have passed but most likely our family and friends will have passed away. It will be you and I starting our family here on the ranch," Joe commented as he sat on his saddle looking down river at the sparse trees and dry grass.

"That is both sad and satisfying. Our leaving is really a final goodbye to our friends that stay here. Our return will provide me with the foundation I want my core family to have," Lydia replied as she leaned across and gave Joe a kiss.

"Let's get back and get the smell of horse sweat removed and get ready for our wedding," Joe said as he turned Yin around and headed for the barn.

The guests had all arrived. Only one of Lydia's friends had declined at the last moment because one of their children had pink eye.

Lunch was just being served when four black helicopters approached Uncle Ted's helo landing area. One of the four landed immediately while the other three hovered in formation. By this time almost the entire gathering was out to see who was arriving.

General Jorge Martinez walked out to the landing area and greeted President MacAdam with a salute and then a hug.

"This is a pleasant surprise," Jorge commented. "Let me introduce you to the father of the groom and the parents of the bride."

"I am referred to as Uncle Ted and I would like to invite you to our pre-wedding luncheon," Uncle Ted offered.

By this time, the President's guards had all descended onto the landing area and were in position.

"The men in black have arrived," Jarret whispered to one of his new cowhand friends.

"Please, help me fit in without disrupting your plans. I offer to preside over the marriage if it complements the event," Lacy said as she shook hands with Joe and Lydia and gave each a hug.

"I will talk with the Mayor of Canadian. I am sure she will be honored to share the limelight with you," Trey commented.

Another Table was quickly set up and serving of lunch continued.

"I am offering to have you run my kitchen at the White House any time you wish," the President later said to Uncle Ted as he made his rounds of the guests.

"We will be listening to this story for a long time," Joe whispered to Lydia when he heard the offer being made.

While the tent arrangement was being transformed into the wedding arrangement, Trey offered to take the President for a tour of the ranch. Trey was very much into the actions of the government and the two seemed to be discussing policy.

"I wonder what kind of help Dad is giving the President," Joe commented to Darian as the two got ready for the wedding.

About an hour later, Joe, Darian, R cubed, and Jarret were all standing up at the altar. They had matching black tuxedos, black boots, and White Stetson hats with black bands.

Uncle Ted sat on a stool and played Canon in D by Pachelbel on his classical guitar. He displayed an amazing touch.

Joe was surprised. Lydia was not wearing the outfit matching his but a white gown. He immediately recognized it as the one his father had kept hanging in the back of the closet. It was the one his mother had worn on her wedding day.

It was a heart-warming surprise. Tears came to his eyes.

"Give me a hanky," he whispered to Darian.

"She is stunning, and the dress is gorgeous," the President whispered from where she stood.

The maid of honor, Lydia's longtime friend stepped forward and arranged the train and flipped back the veil.

"We are not only so very proud of you, but we really like Joe and his family," Lydia's father said as she gave him a kiss and thanked him.

Lydia had a radiant smile as she stepped forward to hold Joe's hands.

The President and the Mayor then led them through the wedding vows and pronounced them husband and wife.

Joe had planned to ride off into the sunset with Lydia at his side, but the white gown changed that slightly and they made a detour to the house to allow Lydia to change out of her gown.

They then came out to ride away on Yin and Yang. They would ride to the river and return for the reception.

The President's helicopter made a low pass and a wag. She was on the way back to Washington and the challenge of leading the most powerful country in the world.

"To be married by the President might be a first. I will have to look it up," Lydia said as they dismounted and stood looking at their swimming hole.

"I think everyone was surprised to see her show up. I did take it as the ultimate in giving positive feedback. "I will have to vote for her in the upcoming election," Joe replied as he leaned into kiss Lydia.

The reception was planned to be that evening. They would leave early the next morning and fly to Kauai.

Jorge had interceded in their plans as to the destination island. He pointed out that Kauai offered better hiking and horseback riding. They were to stay in a house on Hanalei Bay on the northern part of the Island.

"I don't want to ruin your honeymoon but you two know first-hand the actions those opposed to this effort would take if they could," Jorge had told the two when he had informed them of these arrangements.

The General had arranged for the location and the house. It was a large house with a central area and wings out to the side. They would have four guards watching over them and traveling with them throughout their stay.

These guards were the same ones that guarded them on the base.

This made it much easier for Joe and Lydia to accept. By this time, the guards were close to being friends.

There was a very nice beach where they could walk. A paved road ran parallel to the beach. This allowed their guard escorts to guard them but stay out of the way.

The highlight of their honeymoon was their trip around the Napoli Coast on a private catamaran for them and their guards. They stayed on the catamaran for two days and enjoyed the coast, snorkeling and eating freshly caught and grilled fish.

Back on the mainland, the New Year celebrations ended the event at the Ranch.

"Well Ted, you outdid yourself on how you handled all the arrangements. Now all you have to do is get everything back to normal," Trey turned to Ted as the last of the visitors were driven away to the airport.

"I have splurged and hired the cleanup crew. They will return the RV's, take down the tent, straighten out the yard and clean up the house.

Our crew hands love their newly refurbished living area and are helping get that straightened out.

I think all you and I have to do is to sit down on the veranda and enjoy some cookies and a cup of coffee and celebrate the fact that our boy has found the love of his life," Uncle Ted replied as he led the way with a pot of coffee, some cups, and a plate of cookies.

Chapter 21: Launch Preparation

Good preparation normally means the trip goes as desired. Normally people think through what they will be doing and pack their clothes to suit. A famous travel advisor made a comment that there are people that travel light and then there are the people that wish they had traveled light.

The challenge for the Door team was to envision the work and activities they would undertake as they traveled the length of the solar system delivering the Door modules.

Delivery was being designed to be a push of a button. What to do during the time between button pushes was one of the main concerns.

Lydia discussed one possibility with Tom and Linda. Tom highlighted that the problem with the idea was precision. Before they could try it, they would have to prove the precision of the signal delivery over the distances across the solar system. He promised to pursue the idea.

Meanwhile the planning, the launch schedule and the final team preparation became the primary focus for everyone on the team.

"The entire team is qualified on the assembly procedures, and we are continuing the astronaut training.

The zero-gravity practice seems to be the go no go test. Several of the candidates have continued to fail that practice. One has decided to call it quits," Joe shared with the rest of the team.

He and Lydia had been back a week. The intensity of the Door team's work made the honeymoon feel like a long time ago.

"The lift sequence, location and timing have been worked out. General Delaney and his team will inspect all items as they get loaded for lift off," Darian gave his update.

"I will be inspecting and shipping the specified Doors to their specifically designated ship sites and will be the one to inspect them prior to launch," Lydia spoke up next.

"R cubed and I have communicated with each lift off site. The launch sites are the Cape, Arizona, Brazil, China, Russia, India, and Japan.

Israel has offered lift for smaller items since they do not have the larger rockets.

Each site has been designated specific materials to launch and the orbit location in space to place the load. This has been worked with General Delaney and with our own support materials team.

Our team was formed to ensure all the necessary materials for the long-term travel was identified. The team is made up of city planners, industrial planners, and nutritionists and some of our own Door members," Samantha continued the reports.

"Linda and I have been working with all the teams to ensure we are utilizing the Door technology to its fullest. The idea is to utilize several of the orbiting Door modules to transport many of the materials needed for the longer term. This will greatly decrease the time it takes to get all those items into space. It does require we send more of the natural earth up. This actually allows for more efficient launch loading. We will also be sending all but the first group of Doormen and Doorwomen via the Door," Tom added.

"You have heard from several of the teams.

There are several more associated with ground and sea logistics, medical evaluation, and the long term mental and physical health and scientific tests to be conducted during travel. These teams are all on track. I am monitoring all the teams.

You can see the critical path visual in the back of the room. It is all green. Any item falling behind is turned red. I usually take action with the team in question before an item goes red," Ryan said in closing the progress report.

"Thank you. We will now talk about the team make ups for each of the vessels," General Martinez said looking around at the leadership team.

General Delaney had now joined the team as a full member. The rest of the team was made up of Jeffrey Yang from China, Harold Muller from Germany, Manfredo Silva from Brazil, Gupta Kumar from India and Devnid Krupin from Russia, Tom and Linda represented Great Britain and the original Door core team.

This was more team than Jorge liked but it represented the world. Only half the team was physically present. The remaining members were on the screen side of the room.

To Jorge, it always seemed that the least involved asked the most questions.

Jorge had designed his meetings so that those doing the real work would report to the leadership team and then be able to leave.

Jerry, Jacqueline, Aaron, Ryan, and he would sit through the question-and-answer period. This worked well and some of the questions actually did prove to be useful.

"The Doors are all being shipped out this week. They will go by ship to each of our overseas locations.

The ones for the Cape and Arizona will remain here. The demonstrators at the Gate have made it necessary to airlift the Doors out.

The ones for Japan and India will go out of Portland.

The ones for Russia will go out of Houston.

We will move the ones for the Cape at the end of the week and the ones for Arizona will go via helicopter. I have checked each one and they have not been tampered with," Lydia commented to the smaller working team made up of Joe, Darian, Samantha, R cubed and Yara.

"We have ended up with more lift capacity than originally estimated," General Delaney commented in the leadership meeting, "With the lift capacity of China, Japan, India, Brazil, Mexico, Israel, and the US we have enough lift capacity to get all our materials up and do it more quickly.

And Jorge, we cannot use the matter transmitters to lift the shielding material. The material must already be there so the power can utilize it to construct whatever you send. However, we can now send more raw material up and are doing so."

"Well, it seemed logical that night when we were talking over a beer and I suggested it," Jorge said with a smile and a nod.

"We will assign the materials to each launch site based on the logistical and political situation. Here in the US, we have demonstrators at our gates, and they have already set up small contingencies at our two launch facilities. This will not deter us, but we will begin the launches from the other sites first," Jorge commented.

"How is our team selection process going," Jorge asked looking at Jacqueline?

"There seem to be some natural self-selection going on. You all know the six that have just presented to you.

Jeffrey has added three more people from China, and they are all very well matched and are very compatible as a team.

The other teams will need some work, but I am having various combinations of people work together to see how they get along. When team members get to know each other and naturally get along, they reorient and start hanging out together. I do more watching than anything else," Jackie updated the team.

"The program has settled in on six Doorships. There are three of US-EU design, one Brazilian, one Chinese, and one Japanese design. India has one in the works, but it will probably not be ready until later.

The Brazilian ship is the biggest and has been selected to be the first one sent on its way. It will go the farthest out. Jerry and the now combined Doorship team are reviewing all the plans and adjusting them for the quick connect technology Jerry's team developed. This feature will be added to the design of all the Doorships. The need for gravity has resulted in very similar design features.

The Brazilian design is unique in its heavy use of ceramic in its fabrication. There is very little metal in its design. A ceramic powder melting technique will be used to ceramic weld the sections together," Jeffrey Yang reported.

He was now working with Ryan in the planning and the timing of all the launches.

"At the request of several of the Door candidates, we are incorporating gardening facilities. These will be fully functional and capable of providing fresh fruits and vegetables for the crew. This combination will actually help with the long-term conditioning of the air on the Doorships.

The possibility of including small animals was discussed but we came to the conclusion it would potentially be detrimental in the longer term. If we change our minds in the future, we can always transmit them to the ships.

Right Jorge," Jerry shared with the team.

"Right Jerry," Jorge replied with a slight humble bow.

He knew he and Jerry would be exchanging jabs for some time to come about his misdirected advice on shielding.

Lydia went to each launch location to inspect the Door assemblies prior to launch. She would meet the ship the Doors were on. No one was allowed off until she inspected all of the containers and the Door units.

Mexico was the first delivery, and everything cleared.

The deliveries to Brazil and China were repeats.

Then during the inspection for the Russian delivery Lydia discovered that the containers had been opened and the units opened as well.

The entire crew was put under house arrest and the Russian representative arrived with the security police.

"Tom you and Linda need to come and ensure that the systems still work," Lydia informed them on her call back to San Antonio.

"Is there any visible damage," Tom asked?

"I am not sure. There may be a few components missing. It is hard to tell," Lydia replied.

"I will arrange to have a technician capable of fixing the units travel with us. We will leave today," Tom said as he looked at Linda for her concurrence.

The crew denied messing with the containers. Lydia had inspected them on loading, and they had been untouched. Now both of her glue seals on each unit had been broken. Every unit on the ship had been breached. Lydia went through the process of opening the container and then opening each of the units. Just to get in would have taken over an hour.

Someone who knew exactly what to do, could have done it faster. An unfamiliar person would have taken significantly longer.

"Sometime during the transit someone on this crew spent several hours in the hold with the containers. Who would like to make this easy and just confess," Lydia said when she talked to the crew of eight?

The ship was huge, but it was mostly automated and had video cameras everywhere. The video footage was being scanned as she talked. The analysts were looking for the person who was missing from the rest of the crew. They were meticulously putting a timeline to each individual.

During their review, they discovered a ninth person on one of the cameras in the container hold. None of the crew knew anything about such an individual.

An inch-by-inch search of the ship was launched. The crew joined to assist. They wanted the person found so they could get off the hook for the security breach.

The ship's top side was guarded by security police. The dock was also occupied by the army. A Russian patrol boat floated on the opposite side. There were at least one hundred personnel involved.

The person they were looking for had little chance of escape.

It turned out they discovered an extra container. It was a fully self-contained living area. When they burst in the ninth person was sleeping in his bunk. He was surprised to have been discovered since his container was marked with diplomatic insignia and sealed from the outside.

The Ship's Captain had quickly cleared up the issue with the diplomatic insignia by stating that none had been entered in his shipment manifest.

The Russian military had no issue with breaking into the container

"That was a quick trip," Lydia said the next day as she gave Tom and Linda a hug.

"I have moved the units to the launch site and have arranged to have them powered up for testing. You will have to give the OK for the power up," Lydia continued after having been introduced to James, the technician from the builder of the units.

She had worked with him before when she had been inspecting the units during assembly.

"Before we power up anything, I will inspect every circuit and every connection. Most of the system is sealed and has a thick plastic coating. I suspect we will find some missing components or cut wires. I will also inspect all slide connections," James replied.

"I leave this in your hands," Lydia said to Tom and Linda, "I need to get back and inspect the units that are being sent to Arizona and the Cape.

Then I am off to Brazil for launch into space. I hope to see you two there before the launch."

Chapter 22: Blade of Justice

Religious fervor or strong misguided beliefs often result in illogical offensive or deadly actions. This strong negative energy distorts normal logic and instead inserts destructive, self-defeating behavior.

Muhyi al Din Hakimi had long fought against the western devils. When his number one arch enemy had him released from his captivity in Egypt and then sent the message and the information about the launch of the first crew to deliver the "Door" into the heavens, he took this as a message from the heavens.

"God is great," he had repeated multiple times.

It became his passion to deliver a blow against the western devil. He knew that he would fulfill the reason for his name and be the blade of justice. His tactical fighting ability was flawless, his strategic thought process was distorted by his hatred he had for the western infidels.

Mathew Pinkerton III had used his old spy network connections to set up a group of Jihadists connected with the ISIS group. He had reached into the Soviet Union and made the connections that would move missiles capable of hitting any launch site in the western hemisphere into the ISIS held territory.

"Why would my worst enemy provide me with the means to destroy the efforts of his nation," was the first thought that crossed Muhyi al Din Hakimi's mind?

He suspected trickery and treachery.

"You must understand the situation that Mathew Pinkerton III is in. He faces spending the rest of his life in prison.

That situation is due to his hatred for the female President of the United States.

His new purpose in life is the effort to destroy her and her projects," Hakimi's cousin from the US shared with him.

"How will I know when and where the launch is to occur," Muhyi asked his cousin.

"A message will be placed in the Wall Street journal with the information. I will check for it on a daily basis. When the message comes through, I will send you a message about the wonderful figs you gave me and how much I enjoyed them.

The location and co-ordinates will be included in the thank you message. It will be the number and letter after every Arabic character in the message," the cousin replied.

It took Muhyi more than six months to convince his leadership partners that this would be the most significant action that ISIS could take against the Western Devils.

"The US has a weak woman leader. She will cry bloody murder, but we will be sitting on top of a clear world victory," Muhyi said as he finally convinced them.

Six missile launchers capable of reaching any launch site in the world were delivered to them through mysterious channels.

The team that came along with the launchers to provide training were clearly blue eyed and not of the faithful. They were tolerated in order to let the faithful get the training that was needed.

The missile launchers were strategically hidden across the territory ISIS controlled.

Once the training was complete the trainers were immediately asked to leave the area.

There was no leak or indication the West knew about any of the preparation. The systems were brought online but never powered up.

Their wait for the message about the launch location and time was relatively short though it seemed like a lifetime.

"What else can we use the missiles for," was a question that Muhyi raised.

"There are always key cities we can target but these missiles and their destruction delivery method is designed to take down airplanes and other missiles," their weapons expert had explained during the training.

"I will be the one to launch the first missile. It will be my hand that strikes the blow that destroys the she devil's plans," Muhyi thought.

"I will be the Blade of Justice."

Meanwhile back in Florida, the US had its own home-grown terrorists that were ensuring that the information flow would alert the anti-Door contingent.

Madeline had a rather extensive network among computer programmers. Many worked for contractors with contracts with the government. She had contacts among the programmers for the Doorships and she had contacts doing programing at Lakland Air Base.

"How is General Martinez doing," was a question she often asked her contacts?

She would always change her questions slightly, but her goal was to find out when and where the General was or was going.

Finally, she got the reply she had been waiting for.

"He is off to Brazil. I am not sure why, but I heard it was to be at the first Door launch," her contact shared as if everyone in the world already knew this information.

"Thank you for people who like to show that they are in the know," Madeline thought to herself as she listened to her contact talk.

Madeline placed her ad for a maid the next day. She had already done her homework of where all the launch sites were located and had the coordinates for the Brazilian launch site.

"Finally," Muhyi thought as his cousin sent him greeting and thanked him for the dates.

He knew what he was looking for, but it took him more than an hour to extract the co-ordinates from the message. He was impressed with his cousins coding abilities.

Muhyi left the comfort of his quarters in the city and drove out to the missile launch site. He spent the day with his missile crew and programmed in the coordinates of the launch site.

He also ensured the satellite connection to the guidance system was properly functioning. He and his team practiced in setting the target coordinates and the launch sequence for an entire week.

"We will need to be precise and destroy the launch rocket. We must be the blade of justice," Muhyi said as he tried to create enthusiasm in his team.

A lowly US Navy third class IC on one of the destroyers in the Mediterranean recognized the satellite connection to rocket launchers.

He was on a routine monitoring watch. It was a standard procedure to scan the area 360 degrees around the ship and intercept and analyze any electronic activity.

The monitoring range was roughly a thousand miles. The distance was very dependent on the terrain of the land, the strength of the signal being transmitted, and the target object being transmitted to. In the case of a satellite, the coverage range was almost half the world.

"Sir, the ISIS group seems to have some sort of missile launcher located out in the desert," he reported to the officer of the deck.

"Get a lock on it and see what we can learn," the order came back.

The coordinates of the site were logged, and the information was sent up the chain of command. There was nothing to do at the time, but it might be intel that would later be critical.

Chapter 23: A family Affair

Sometimes the punishment does not fit the crime. Mathew was not being rehabilitated, he was not suffering, he was flourishing in an environment conducive to his goals. The low security "Prison" he was in featured a two-mile-long walking trail, a gym, a library, and an entertainment room. It was an ideal environment that provided him food, security, and a relaxed atmosphere that he leveraged.

Sure, his room was tiny, but he only slept there. The rest of the time Mathew was up and about enjoying himself and plotting his revenge.

He actually felt less stress than at any time in his life that he could remember. He thought about the childhood story of Brer Rabbit and the briar patch. He chuckled to himself as he realized that his enemy had inadvertently put him in an ideal place to plan his revenge.

The guards seemed inept. He willingly accepted their direction but always made it a point to circuitously slight and insult them. They seemed too dumb to catch on.

He was quite satisfied with himself.

He had set revenge plans A, B and C into action. He was quite sure one of the three would be successful.

"Lacy won't know what hit her and from where," he thought to himself as he walked rigorously on the outdoor black topped trail that went around the grounds of the low security prison.

"I only wish I could watch when the missile takes out the launch of the crew heading up into space. I bet that will frost her puss" Mathew continued his musing.

He stopped his walking to look skyward and image the missile approaching the rocket as it went up into the air. It was a clear to him as if he was on the missile as it approached the launch rocket.

He and Madeline, his grandniece, met once a month. They would take this same walk and talk about the progress being made. Madeline made all the arrangements for each of the plans. She seemed to relish that part of the effort.

"Make sure you don't leave a trail," Mathew had warned her.

"It will be very hard for them to connect me. I have done nothing directly, so my fingerprint is invisible," Madeline replied.

She was really quite pleased with her ability to stay invisible. This activity had re-invigorated her life. It had given her purpose.

"You seem to have found new energy," her boyfriend had commented.

"Yes, my current project at work has been quite fun," had been her reply.

Her boyfriend was also a new item in her life. She was now enjoying herself. Her single goal was to stick it to the President. She wished she could share what was going on with someone other than Great Uncle Mathew.

She certainly could not share it with her current boyfriend. Besides, she was really not into him in a serious way. She just liked the attention and the nighttime trysts.

The programing of an invisible and as much as possible undetectable bug became a major part of Madeline's daily thoughts. She wished she could claim to have designed the perfect Trojan horse bug that she passed on to her contact on the Door programing team.

She belonged to a computer programmer's club called "Hackers." She challenged them to design a simple routine that would take down any computer. The club members really got into it and had a contest to determine who could come up with the simplest routine that would take the least number lines or commands. She was in the competition and her entry was near the top, but the winner had fifty fewer code elements.

It was the winning routine that she had put into the Door program.

She was impressed with its simplicity.

Madeline kept track of the Door team. This she did through her fairly broad network of programing friends.

She had struck up a friendship with Great Uncle Mathew's contractor friend Victor.

Victor was well to do and had a yacht in Miami. Madeline enjoyed the cruises or just relaxing on the boat as it remained anchored at the dock.

It was a platonic relationship.

Victor was always accompanied by some glamorous young lady or "body" as he referred to them. He and Madeline enjoyed the political discussions and conversations about world affairs.

Their common dialogue was to rant about the stupid actions and the works of the President. They each seemed to be able to constantly repeat the same trash line as if it were fresh and new.

"The order for soil to be sent up has increased dramatically. There must be a change in plans. I am processing ten times the original order. It will probably be closer to a thousand times more soil by the time we get done," Victor shared during one of their evening dinner sessions.

"I have no clue why they would need more soil" Madeline replied.

"I don't either, but all the latest orders have been sent to Brazil. This probably means that will be the first launch," Victor continued.

"That confirms what I have learned," Madeline said as a surge of energy went through her. Her own sleuthing had pointed to Brazil as well.

"All the extra soil has made it easier to send up the doctored soil. Each load is packaged as a bound unit. I learn the specific placement in a few days," Victor continued.

"I will send the message to those who are waiting for the location of the prepared soil as soon as you have it," Madeline replied.

She was to place an ad with this information in the Miami Herald in the lost and found section.

"I have known Mathew a long time. There must be at least two or three other sabotage plans in place," Victor made a statement in hopes of finding out more about them.

"Victor, you know that if I told you, I would be responsible for getting you shot," Madeline replied with a line she always heard and then gave a small laugh.

"It's great to have the whole picture and have people like Victor asking for it," Madeline thought to herself as she sipped on the excellent red wine that Victor had served.

These moments re-invigorated her and made her body tingle.

She was aware of the continuing demonstration at the Lakland gates. She hoped it made the President worry.

Madeline's Uncle Samuel was the person orchestrating the demonstrators. Most of the demonstrators were paid to do it. Uncle Samuel was a through and through racist, but Madeline noticed he was able to put this bias aside. The crowd at the gate was a mix of Asian, Blacks, Hispanics, and Whites.

"Uncle Samuel knows how to set the scene for the media," Madeline thought as she watched the news.

Madeline saw that the media was displaying a totally integrated opposition to the Door effort. This was absolutely a false message to all of the country and the world.

Samuel had been called on to testify in Mathew's trial. He had refused to directly link his actions to anything coming from Uncle Mathews.

"I am not sure how I got that information. I did my own reconnaissance two weeks before I set up the demonstration at the gate. The invites were sent to people who have previously demonstrated against unreasonable government activities" Uncle Samuel had testified.

The timing was of course checked out and confirmed his testimony.

He had refused to provide any other information and he continued to keep the demonstration at the gates going.

He used the news media to support Uncle Mathew and the right of the people of the USA to demonstrate against the oppression of the government.

"This whole trial of Mathew is political, biased and a lie," Samuel said as he looked into the news camera.

All of his actions, though very biased and with little merit, were legal and guaranteed by the US Constitution.

"This is truly a family affair. I wonder how this is going to look in the long run. A family of crazies or the family that changed the course of history," Madeline thought as she sipped her wine and enjoyed the sunset.

As far as Madeline could tell, everything was in place and set to succeed. She kept examining each scenario and felt that she was on the winning side.

All the planned actions seemed bullet proof.

"I will probably never know if the Trojan horse snipped would have worked. I wish it was the first not the last sabotage effort," she thought to herself as she dried off from her shower and got ready for a good night's sleep.

Chapter 24: Launch

Anticipation of a major event is often followed by a letdown afterwards. The launch of the first crew that would begin a journey to the edge of the solar system had a great deal of anticipation and stress associated with it.

The crew and large cast of supporters were ready for a letdown. The intensity they had been experiencing was hard to maintain. Burn out of almost everyone was clearly visible.

The anticipation was felt around the world.

Mathew lay awake the entire night imagining the events of plan A.

Muhyi attended several additional prayers pledging his allegiance to Allah for letting him be the Blade of Justice.

Victor enjoyed his two floozies and partied most of the night. He was not so much into anticipation as into worry about traceability. He was hoping Madeline was as invisible as she thought she was.

The following month the launch of materials began.

China began launching slightly ahead of Brazil. Soon all sites were launching and placing the materials into space. All the parts needing assembly were launched first.

Finally, it was time for the first Doormen to be launched.

Joe, Lydia, Darian, Samantha, R cubed and Yara were scheduled to be the first team to go up. They would launch from the site in Brasilia and would begin their assembly first. Their goal was to evaluate the assembly approach they had practiced. The assembly, based on their practice, would take approximately two months.

Trey, Uncle Ted, Lydia's parents, Jarret, Darian, and Samantha's parents all took vacation in Brazil. They all flew into Sao Paulo. Once there, they were escorted and guided around by Yara's parents. They were all going to see a little of the city. Then they would take in Rio de Janeiro and then they would go to Brasilia for the launch.

The Door team did not have the luxury of time, so Yara gave them the whirlwind tour with one day at each location. They got to the top of Sugar Loaf Mountain by helicopter. The helicopter had jet power for its forward motion. It could go into full helicopter mode when necessary. This was their private transport that eventually delivered them to the Brasilia launch area.

"That was the fastest cross-country tour I have ever experienced," Samantha joked to Yara as they approached Brasilia.

"Yes, I didn't know Brazil was so small," R cubed joined in. He knew Yara was proud of Brazil being one of the largest countries in the world and that recently it had achieved the status a top-level world player.

"Be happy that you will be on the best ship of them all. It is made in Brazil, and it is a green ship," Yara rebutted.

She was proud that Brazil had built the ceramic based ship versus a metal based one. It would be the ship that would last the longest. It was selected to be the one to leave the solar system for that specific reason.

The day before the launch all the family members shared an evening meal at an upscale churrascaria. This particular one also specialized in sushi. This was a favorite for Yara's family.

Jorge and the leadership team were there as well. They had taken over the entire facility for the event.

The area was heavily guarded by the Brazilian Army. This was a proud moment for Brazil and the Brazilians were not taking any chances. Their security was at its height.

At the last moment, Linda and Tom had made it in from Russia.

Over dinner Tom let the team know the status of the Doors in Russia, "James, the technician, has called in a team to check every circuit and function of the Doors. He and his team will let us know when they are ready for us to test the Doors. He found all the connectors had been ruined. He had a totally new set of electronics and circuit boards shipped out for each of the units."

"He will refurbish the damaged ones later and will install them on the units being prepared for the Earth hospitals. Those components would never get into space.

We are not needed until they get the units back to specification."

"Tomorrow afternoon will see the start of the Door delivery effort. We are sending up the first team. This team is first in many ways. Three members were the first humans to be transmitted. They have led the training and development of the other members. They have been instrumental in eliminating barriers and problems. They certainly are first among all of us," Jorge concluded his toast.

The countdown for launch was to start at ten in the morning with a launch at three in the afternoon. There was no fanfare, but the President of both Brazil and the US called and addressed the team.

"You are my sweetheart team. Make the world proud," President MacAdam said briefly.

"Brazil is proud to have a representative on the first team and to be host to the first launch," the Brazilian President added.

Brazil had been launching load after load for at least a month. They would have been out of lift rockets, but Ryan and R cubed had positioned all the lift capacity based on the material to be launched. It had taken since the previous summer to get all of it in place.

Russia, China, and Japan had each said they had enough of their own lift capacity in place. Mexico and Brazil needed launch capacity added. The US had distributed all of its extra capacity to the North America and Latin America launch sites.

Finally, the time came when the six team members walked to the nose cone module. It was designed to take the six up and then attach to a section of what would become one of the six modules for the Doorship. This section had the control center for the Doorship and the shielded living area.

Joe and Darian had qualified in the control of the launch module. Their qualification was a back-up precaution. The entire launch and flight sequence was totally automated. The team entered the module, seated, and buckled themselves in. They were all in their flight suits. These suits were meant only for the launch and designed for lighter work. These suits provided the maximum flexibility.

Everyone had another heavy-duty assembly space suit. These other suits were designed to be more rugged and provide an environment that allowed for longer term usage when doing work in space. These suits were located in the main control module and had been launched with the module.

Joe and Darian went methodically through the pre-launch check-off.

The countdown began thirty minutes later and proceeded without any problems or delays.

Jorge and all the other team members sat on bleachers shaded by a covering looking out at the launch pad.

"There they go. God speed," Jorge commented to those around him.

A Camera crew was transmitting the view of the rocket rising smoothly into the sky above a trail of white vapor. The rocket dropped its launch section and the booster stage kicked in.

"All readings are normal, and the launch is proceeding with no problems," a voice from the control room announced.

Halfway around the world another rocket launched from somewhere in the Middle East. It was immediately tracked by a US Navy carrier in the region.

"Missile launch from eastern Syria or perhaps northern Iraq. Trajectory appears to be toward the Brasilia launch location," the message went out from the carrier to the high command.

"We have been informed of an incoming missile apparently targeting our launch," one of the launch support announced in an excited voice to the Door team in the module.

"How long to impact," Joe inquired?

His mind was immediately racing as he decided what to do.

"We have about eleven minutes," was the reply.

"How long until booster module separation," Joe asked next?

"Module separation is to be in fifteen," was the reply.

"How long is the separation burn to last," Joe continued his inquiry?

"The separation burn is to last for two minutes," was the reply.

"I am taking manual control, NOW," Joe said as he flipped the control switch to manual.

"I want you to give me a thirty second warning before missile impact.

I doubt it is intended to actually impact us. Instead, it will explode just prior to reaching us and send out shrapnel in a pattern something like a shot gun.

I will manually fire the separation rockets and keep them active until they are totally used. You all figure how long it will take us to get to the orbiting module," Joe informed the control center.

"We will give you the warning," was the immediate reply.

"Team, stay strapped in, keep calm, pray," Joe said as he reviewed his practice manual control experience in his mind.

"Darian back me up. Let's make sure we keep the rockets active until they run out of fuel. Lydia you are the designated medic on this launch, be ready in case someone needs attention," Joe slowly and methodically gave his commands.

A moment later ground control came back with the bad news, "even using all the separation rocket fuel this will not be enough to take you up to the module. You will be somewhere in the neighborhood of a soccer field short of the orbiting module altitude."

"Damn, does anyone have a good idea on how to close that gap," Joe commented on the closed circuit in the module?

"We each have a fifty-foot line for our space walks. This comes close to the distance we will need to reach the module. The six lines can be joined and one of us can float toward the module. If the float is correctly aim that person will either be at the module or close enough, they could detach and use exhaust air to propel them to the module.

Once there, they could enter and find more line and attach that to the line they pulled over from this capsule," Lydia made her suggestion in rapid order.

"Missile Impact in thirty seconds," suddenly rang in all their ears.

Joe immediately counted to three and triggered the separation of the capsule from the booster. The separation was like the acceleration of a drag race car. Everyone was pulled back into their seats.

"OK, everyone hang on and pray that we get beyond the pattern of the blast," Joe said through gritted teeth.

The module kept accelerating beyond its designated speed to the point the entire interior was vibrating. Joe continued to push the system to its limit.

The incoming rocket approached, and the ground radar showed the booster rocket being ripped apart by the shrapnel. It was exactly as Joe had predicted.

Joe kept the rockets firing until they ran out of fuel.

Suddenly a piece of shrapnel punched a hole through the back of the module, glanced off Darian's helmet, and hit the control panel and lodged itself in what had been the visual display. A fine spray pattern of broken glass made its way across the chamber of the capsule.

Lydia released the straps holding her to her chair and quickly placed the control instruction binder over the hole created by the shrapnel and sealed it with foam sealing gel. The foam hardened and the hole was sealed.

"Are you OK," Yara asked Darian in a tone of concern.

"Yes, I am lucky I was slouching down in fear," Darian quipped as he ran his gloved hand along the groove cut across his helmet.

"I'm also very glad they made the helmet good and thick," he continued.

"Brasilia, how are we doing," Joe inquired after the firing stopped?

"We are cheering like crazy down here. We did not think you would be able to survive," came exuberant the reply.

"You will come up short on reaching the target space module. "We are working on how to get you there," ground control continued.

Jorge was transmitting the conversation between ground control and the Door team.

"Yes, Door team, way to go," Tom said excitedly when the immediate survival of the team was confirmed!

"OK, I am going to go across as Lydia suggested. I will push off toward the module. If I see that I am properly aligned I will unbuckle myself at the last moment. If I am not in line pull me back in and I will try again," Joe said as he moved to open the capsule hatch.

"That won't work," Samantha spoke up.

"If you push off, you will go toward the target space module, but we will be going equally away from it. Half of the line will be used up by us and half by you. You will come up significantly short. We will then be pulled back toward each other. If you disconnect, we will float away," Samantha continued.

"Yes, that was quick thinking. We almost committed a fatal novice error," R cubed chimed in.

"Yes, thank you. We have two fire extinguishers. Can we use them to propel one of us over," Yara suggested?

"That will have to do. It will be somewhat slower. We will still need to pull the line across as far as it will reach," Joe commented.

He felt irritated with himself for almost creating a catastrophe. The action and reaction would not be quite as extreme as Samantha had stated but non-the-less it was a correct call.

Lydia connected all the lines together. Joe exited the module. He hooked the fire extinguishers to two loops on his space suit. He snapped the line into another ring on his waist.

He had to resist the temptation to push off from the capsule. Instead, he aimed the fire extinguisher in the opposite direction of the line he envisioned to the orbiting module. The exhausting fire extinguisher looked just like a small rocket exhaust.

"You are looking good. You are moving slowly and that is good. I am feeding out the line as smoothly as possible. I will let you know when I have only a few loops left," Lydia was saying to Joe.

"Joe, you need a minor direction adjustment. You need to point the fire extinguisher at my left shoulder and give it a short burst," Lydia informed Joe.

"Ok, here goes," Joe replied.

"That's good. It looks like a strike across home plate," Lydia responded.

"Looking good, looking good, looking good, you are on the last loop. Disconnect," was her running string of comments.

Joe did as instructed. It was almost a perfect disconnect, and the line hung in space as he continued his backward journey.

"I think you have almost reached the module. Can you spin around and face it," Lydia inquired?

Joe made a very small burst of the extinguisher across his chest. He indeed did spin around but he also got a sideward drift. Luckily for him it was a drift along the axis of the module.

He hit the structure hard enough to bounce back but he put his hands out in front of him and caught the frame of the module as he bounced back.

He pulled himself slowly along the module to its entry hatch. It was a chamber style entry. He sealed the outer hatch. He was then able of fill the chamber with air and opened the inner door.

He immediately began to look for additional cable or tethers. He went to the spacesuit storage area and found the additional tethers that were needed. He exchanged the used fire extinguisher for a new one.

"I am now glad at all the hours we spent in the pool simulating our movements out in space," Joe thought to himself.

Joe stopped at the control consul and turned on the communication system and the video monitoring system. He wanted to let the ground team hear and see what was happening.

"Ground Control this is Door One command. Do you copy," Joe asked?

"Yes, you are loud and clear," the same voice that had given him the thirty second warning replied.

"You should have a video feed, now," Joe said as he flipped the video transmit switch on.

"Affirmative all cameras are online. Thank you for thinking of this," came back to Joe.

Joe returned to the entry chamber and exited the orbiting module. He attached the cable to the module.

Everyone in the control room and the observers at the observation area were silent.

At the White House, a pin would have been heard if dropped.

"Ok Lydia I am ready to come back. I am going to aim for the module. Let me know what adjustment I should make. The goal is to get me back to the end of the line I pulled over," Joe spoke quietly in his helmet.

"That's it Joe. You and Lydia are a team," Uncle Ted said quietly to those sitting around him.

"I will guide you to the end of the tether line. Take your time we will do this in short bursts," Lydia replied.

"We have the best out there at the moment," Jorge added.

Lydia adjusted Joe three times.

Finally, he saw the tether line pass nearby. He used one short burst of the extinguisher to push him into the line. He was past the end by about thirty feet. He was ecstatic about getting that close. He pulled on the cable attached to the orbiting module and moved himself to the end of the line going out to the space capsule.

An old-fashioned square knot secured the two lines.

"We can't pull the capsule to the module because we have no way to stop it. You all get out of the capsule. Leave the line connected to the capsule but pull yourselves along the line to the orbiting module.

Come in slowly. Once we are all here, we will all go through the entry chamber. It will accommodate two of us at a time," Joe instructed.

The going was slow but about an hour later the team was safely in the module. Joe was the last to enter.

After some brief hugging all around Joe went over to the command center.

"Brasilia, we are all on board the orbiting space module. Our capsule is still floating a football field away," Joe called via the communication equipment in the module.

"There is cheering, and the champagne is flowing. The Phoenix has risen from the ashes," the reply came back.

In the background the cheering and celebrating could be heard.

"I don't know if we have enough champagne out here, but the celebration will go on as long as you want," Jorge said as the champagne glasses were passed out. The popping of the corks followed immediately.

"We must go out and celebrate this occasion. Let's hope the other launches don't take us so low and then take us to the other extreme," Jeffrey commented as he raised his glass high in the familiar toast salute.

Chapter 25: Reprisal

*U*nexpected reprisal is usually devastating in nature. One moment a positive surge of adrenaline, the next moment the oblivion of darkness. This was what Muhyi hoped to be inflict on his target objective.

The saying is do not throw stones if you live in a glass house. He did not know or understand that concept.

If you are walking past a huge paper hornet's nest do not throw stones. The hornets that come out follow the path through the air taken by the stone back to the thrower. He had not ever experienced that.

If you shoot a missile a quarter of the way around the world there is a long, hot signature path. Worse yet is when the signature path is not needed because your location has previously been recorded. This was totally invisible to him.

Muhyi al Din Hakimi was waiting for confirmation of his success. He knew the missile had gone toward the target as expected and had blown the target out of the sky. His crew was cheering, that the Blade of Justice had successfully delivered its blow.

Then the reprisal left a large slag lined hole in the sand.

President MacAdam had listened and watched the entire launch event from her situation room. The entire cabinet and a few other leaders were there with her. They actually had the best view of everything that went on. The control room, the module, and the observation area each were displayed on a separate screen. The ultimate down and dismay and the outright cheering followed the ebb and flow of the launch sequence of events.

"I want an armed missile to back track the trajectory of the attacking rocket. Take out the launcher now," President MacAdam had ordered even before the missile heading toward the Door launch rocket exploded.

The trajectory was in the territory controlled by ISIS. It appeared the launch site was almost exactly on the border of Syria and Iraq.

"Target every missile launch site in the territory controlled by ISIS. Take them all out as well," President MacAdam then ordered.

She did not need any additional authorization. She was the commander in chief of the most powerful country on Earth and sworn to protect its citizens.

A missile launching submarine in the Mediterranean immediately did as ordered.

The blade of justice has decapitated the serpent," Muhyi said as the tracking system signaled a direct hit.

He was sitting cheering the result with his crew when the missile from the submarine exploded and evaporated the launch site.

In the following hour five more missile sites were evaporated. The missile launch capacity delivered by the Russians to ISIS ceased to exist.

President MacAdam went on the air immediately.

"Today, after being attacked in space I ordered the destruction of missile launching sites in the territory currently in the control of ISIS. I will take all actions and steps necessary to protect our country and our citizens from the aggressive actions taken by the rogues that control ISIS," the President informed the nation in a special address.

I ordered the pre-emptive destruction of all other known missile launch sites with similar capabilities. Those leading ISIS should understand that any additional aggressive action on their part will be severely dealt with," President MacAdam said in her address to the nation.

The ISIS leadership had not expected such an immediate and high-level reprisal. They were surprised at President MacAdam's response. They had misjudged her to be weak. They still could not accept a woman as the top world leader. Now, however, they were clear that she was tough and immediately decisive.

ISIS's response was to send missiles into Israel. Israel's missile defense system neutralized every incoming missile.

Each missile was back tracked, and a reprisal missile fired from one of the US submarines. Another three known launch locations were immediately eliminated. After a dozen missiles the ISIS capability seemed to have been neutralized. They stopped firing.

"We were able to trace where their command-and-control center seems to be," one of the Joint Chiefs commented in his discussion with the President.

"Take it out," President MacAdam replied calmly.

"That is an act of war," the General replied.

"General, I believe we have had an open declaration of war with this group for the last twenty years. Order the command center eliminated," the President firmly replied.

She failed to understand the hesitation by the top brass to take action when it was necessary, and this was the right time.

The Kurds took advantage of the situation to mount an attack to retake their territory. They ran into stiff resistance but made steady progress in retaking their previous territory.

Iran followed immediately in advancing against ISIS in its territory. Within the week ISIS had lost both of its Iraqi and Iranian territories.

In the following months, the Syrian army made gains against the last areas held by ISIS. Everything gained by ISIS in the past twenty years unraveled almost instantaneously. The people they had subdued did nothing to help the radicals that had made their lives miserable.

"It looks like the conditions on Earth continue to evolve in the right direction," R cubed commented.

"I hope it does, but the Middle East is still one hundred years behind the rest of the world in treating everyone as equals," Yara commented.

President MacAdam's popularity soared. It was clear that her Door program and her handling of ISIS had almost reassured a second term for her. She was still fighting with some of her own party members, but she was forging a new party alliance that would greatly strengthen their position in both the house and the senate.

The demographics of the country had changed. The successful leader needed the ability to forge alliances with women, the Black, Asian, and Hispanic communities to gain the support needed to control the politics of the country. The President seemed to have mastered these interfaces and had a majority support in each of the groups.

"Well team, I have just talked with the President," Jorge commented as he held his continuing weekly progress meeting. "She wants to thank us for our contributions to her success. And to Joe she sends special regards. She said she was on the edge of her seat yelling go, go, go, when you were pulling off your miraculous escape from the missile attack.

Then she listened in for the entire time while the team was getting to safety. She said she had tears in her eyes and was hooting and hollering like a young schoolgirl when you all got to safety."

"Well tell her we were celebrating ourselves and we appreciate her concern. We all really support her immediate response to the missile attack, and we extend thanks to those sending the retaliating missiles," Joe replied.

"Bravo for the President," Joe said.

The team spent the next few days organizing and determining what to do about their dead capsule. It was supposed to be docked in its docking station and be a safety valve in case of an emergency.

"We can slowly pull it over to the docking area, but we will need to be super careful," Samantha said.

"Perhaps our fire extinguishers can be used as the thrusters. Once we get it docked it will be out of the way and usable though it will not have any propulsion," R cubed commented.

"We will also need to repair and clean up the damage," Yara added.

"I am sure we can get more fuel sent up," R cubed continued in what was more of a relief conversation than anything else.

It was important to get everything in the right place. There were five major modules to be moved into position. The cross members would be erected, and then transmit-receive modules would be sent up. The space around the Door Ship modules had multiple bundles of supplies that needed to be pulled in and loaded into designated modules. The team had come up knowing they had about three months of concentrated assembly and storage work to do.

"We should arrange for the propulsion fuel be sent up on one of the next shots," Adrian suggested.

"I agree with Samantha. The cable is still attached to the capsule. One of us can return to the capsule and attach the cable to its docking point. The cable at this end can be centered in the docking connection.

The person on the module can then make minor corrections with the extinguisher to bring the module exactly into position.

Once we get it docked, we can proceed with our other assembly as planned," Joe said as the team continued to discuss their situation.

Chapter 26: Assembly and Preparation

Plug and play implies something easy to assemble and put into working order. The assembly of a spaceship in the vacuum of space by a team of six people would seem to be impossible.

Jerry Delaney' design team had designed a plug and play spaceship. The assembly of the Doorship was unique in its simplicity. A cable was attached to the outer edge of the mating sections. The sections were pulled together by the single cable. A round protruding nub mated with a matching dimple depression. A shorter cable was attached on the inner edge to pull that edge in to a similar nub and dimple. At this point, the two sections were loosely held together.

A similar process then took place on the other end of the unit and the next section was positioned. This process went on until all six units were loosely attached.

"Well, this is our first assembly milestone. All the sections of Doorship One have been connected," Joe reported during the weekly leadership meeting.

The cross members were all positioned and then the final cable tightening of the entire structure was executed. Each joint was inspected, and the welding robots were brought out and positioned at their starting positions.

Rotation was initiated by ceremoniously firing the small rockets. The station began its counterclockwise rotation. The feeling of gravity slowly built until the team was easily walking on the outer wall and what would from then on be considered down. In reality the force should have been thought of as outward.

The internal walls at the end of each section were removed by twisting the quick disconnect pins one half turn counterclockwise. The onboard team took their first walk around the perimeter together. Each section was roughly the length of a football field and the total distance around was almost exactly a mile. There were living spaces, workspaces, gardens, and storage spaces distributed around the wheel.

"The ship structure is now complete, and the welding started," Joe declared at the next scheduled team meeting.

"Congratulations," Jorge had responded.

"We have been sending up additional reconstitution materials as requested. Each payload has been topped off as requested. Where are you putting it all," General Delaney inquired?

"For now, we are attaching it to the frame of Doorship One. Later we will move it into the garden space and any vacant area we see will hold the equivalent of an additional flower bed. "We want to thank Linda and Tom in working with us to create the opportunity for flow to and from the Doorships," Samantha replied.

Lydia had pursued a different model for the door delivery team. She had a vision where the team members could transmit home and spend significant periods of time on Earth and then transmit back to the Doorship.

"Why if we can transmit to and from, must we remain on the Doorship at all times," She had inquired?

"It is only a matter of having enough material and energy at each end," Tom had replied.

"Then let's plan on having enough material and energy at each end. Wouldn't you like to deliver some of your doors," Lydia had countered?

"That is a great idea. Yes, I would love to deliver some of my own doors," Linda had enthusiastically replied.

"This certainly changes the requirements for those who want to participate. A more fluid environment would allow a different level of involvement. We might even consider sending some personnel focused on special projects," Jacqueline added.

"The energy on the Doorships and the orbiting units will be provided by small nuclear reactors and will last for the lifetime of the project. Having enough reconstitution material has always been the issue. Every launch now going up is topped off with the reconstitution material. This is basically a dense mass of soil," General Delaney continued.

"We have worked with the design team to design membrane covers for the space between the spokes of the Doorship. This provides a huge space for the reconstitution material. We will load all we can get before departure. Then as we capture more material in space, these areas can be filled in," R cubed reported.

"Well, I have heard from every member of the team. Each would like to have a stint on one of the Doorships. We will need to set up a specific protocol as to who gets to go out to the Doorships and who gets to go out to the exploratory Transmit-Receive stations. The original protocol had only the Doormen and later exploratory team members making the transit," Aaron interjected.

"Our capabilities seem to be getting ahead of our mission plans and protocol. Let's spend the next few weeks revisiting this area and coming up with a new understanding of the situation and how we plan to address it," Jorge closed the meeting.

"Well, Lydia, you certainly have stirred up the team," Joe said as he gave her a hug.

"I am thinking about our lives and our family. I want our children to ride on your ranch to know Uncle Ted and your Dad and I want us to open up the solar system. To have both we will need a different work arrangement," Lydia said giving Joe a kiss.

The Doors were launched, and each unit was attached to the specified location on one of the cross members. This was dangerous and tedious work all in one. The team kept stressing safety and safe behaviors. The units they were moving into place weighed several tons. It was easy to forget the physics of the situation. This would be what would be considered the dangerous grunt work.

Doorship One would leave orbit with twelve Doors. This was more than any other Doorship would take. They would deliver one door to the Moon and one door to Mars. Then they would deliver no more doors in the solar system. Their load was slated to go beyond the solar system.

The practice sessions back on Earth had paid off. Each unit was maneuvered into place and moved almost exactly as practiced. The only difference was they were moving at less than half the speed at which they had practiced.

Joe had insisted they do it very slowly. Each unit was close to five thousand pounds.

Getting the doors into space was using up every bit of existing lift capacity and all that was on a rush production schedule. One economist projected a five percent growth in GNP across the World based just on the launch of the Doors.

Lydia also made sure that Doorship One would depart with a full load of reconstitution material. She kept after the ground crew to maximize the load. Every ounce counted. They managed to get one hundred ten percent fill. Lydia moved the extra material into the garden areas.

"Yara, Samantha and I have been working on a work cycle that would allow each of us, two at a time to spend a month back on earth every quarter. We will add two more people so that the ship always has a full complement," Lydia reported.

"That sounds like a great approach. I am looking forward to my turn," Jorge replied.

After the meeting Joe got his team together.

"We have three days to departure. I want us to inspect every inch of Doorship One. I want us to inspect every control system and control instruction. I want every possible point of sabotage to be inspected. We will do an outside and inside inspection. Even the dirt we had sent up is to be inspected. Check its chemical composition," Joe instructed.

It was clear to everyone that Joe was giving orders and it was not a discussion point.

"What makes you feel so strongly about this," Lydia asked for the rest of the team?

She knew by Joe's manner that something was bothering him.

"We have been the unprepared targets in the other attempts to stop us. I would like to get ahead of the next attempt. There are enough people out there with crazy ideas that some additional attempts to interfere with this effort may have been planned," Joe replied.

"Darian and I will take the outside of the hull and the soil storage area," Yara volunteered.

"Samantha and I will take the inside inspection. Why don't the two of you figure out how to check the control system and computer logic," R cubed spoke up next.

He had no interest in trying to understand all the logic that had been thrown into the control system.

"Alright, we will do that," Joe replied.

He knew he would have to engage the ground team to do a thorough analysis of the control systems and their logic. He hoped he would not get any resistance from that area.

"Let's call Jorge, Jerry, Tom and Linda and get them involved as well," Lydia suggested.

This will make sure we get some really deep penetration of the control system. There may be a lot that is beyond us.

"Ok, Joe what did you have in mind," Tom led off the meeting that had been called.

"I want us to diagram the logic of every function and verbally explain it. If possible, the person who did the programing would do this. Are they all available," Joe replied and inquired?

"I can make them available if that is what you are asking for," Jorge and Jerry both replied in unison.

"Yes, that is what I am asking. Also are all the control systems on all the Doorships the same," Joe inquired?

"Not exactly, the three managed by the US, EU, and LA and the Brazilian one are exactly the same. The one from China has different logic as does the one from Japan," Jeffrey Yang spoke up.

He was intrigued and impressed by the precaution that Joe was taking. He would also have the control system on the Chinese Doorship checked out by his team.

"What makes you suspect foul play," Jeffrey inquired?

"I am getting tired of escaping the attacks. I would like to be the one that takes action first and has my counterattack ready.

I cheered President MacAdam's swift and comprehensive response, but it was a response not pre-emptive. We were lucky.

I want to be the eagle that says to the vulture, "I am not going to wait, I am going out and kill something," Joe replied.

"Remind me not to get into a scrape with Joe," one of the young program engineers chimed in.

"You are so right. Everyone who attacked him is either in jail or dead," Linda volunteered to the ground crew.

After two days the team had found nothing.

Then two findings validated Joe's feeling.

"We have a positive result in our soil sample. We randomly took ten samples per storage areas. One sample in one storage area is giving a positive indication of being mixed to be an explosive. We are going to sample the area around the positive sample. And we are going to collect additional samples from all the other areas," Yara reported on the morning of the third day.

"How would the explosive be triggered," Jorge inquired?

An army explosive expert was brought in to evaluate the situation.

"The bomber must have enough information about the placement of the soil to be able to target it with a laser to set it off. That is the only means we have found for the activation of the explosive mixture," he later informed the team.

"Then we are looking for someone involved in the preparation and loading of the soil. Let's figure out who is involved and see it we can learn how they plan to set off the bomb," Jorge said as he looked at Doug.

"Let's neutralize the area and see if we can back track the laser when it gets fired to trigger the explosion," Joe said to the team.

"Also, we can set up a laser of our own and have it set up so it will automatically target the source of the laser back on earth," Yara suggested.

"We found an anomaly in the environmental control system," the designer located in Europe reported. "There seems to be a self-replicating module. Once activated it would self-replicate continuously until it saturated the computer operating system. This would not only shut down the environmental control system but potentially the entire computer."

"I will have my guys program a bypass circuit. We will set up a monitoring circuit to watch for any sign of someone checking on or triggering this function," Jerry spoke up next.

"Let's design a bypass and then see if we can send a Trojan horse back along the activate signal to see if we can trace the culprit. "Do we have some programmers with these kinds of skills," Jorge inquired?

"Yes, we have one individual who can do this to anyone that his computer can connect with. He challenges our system on a periodic basis. It's his job to find the chinks in our armor. He is the one that spotted this one," the head of the Door programing unit replied.

"Let's see if there is some way to determine who the culprits in both these cases happen to be.

I want everyone involved with preparing the soil material for launch investigated.

Additionally, I want everyone who has had access to the control systems be checked out. We will see if we can nab these groups," Jorge spoke up.

"I am having every Doorship thoroughly checked out. I am also activating our militaries to be prepared to retaliate against the laser bombers," Jorge informed the team.

"I will contact my government as well and ask them to be prepared for action," Jeffrey Yang chimed in. Jeffrey knew his government had the capability, but he was not sure they would act as decisively as the US President.

Chapter 27: Door Ship One Departure

Distributed, supportive, developmental leadership is rare. The team onboard Doorship One was such an occurrence.

Joe Pender Elsinger, a shy Texan cowboy, was an unlikely candidate to nurture such leadership behavior. He, however, had a natural belief in the capability of each individual. He was a nurturer and developer of his own capabilities and a believer that everyone would seek to do the best they could.

The people around him were pulled to him in an organic, natural way and they were soon supporting him as he in turn supported them.

People at every level gravitated to the bed rock of leadership Joe exuded. Joe repeatedly pulled off resounding success from what initially appeared to be a stumble, fall or a situation of impending doom.

Joe kept coming out a winner.

A few days later Doorship One was ready for its departure. They were getting underway two weeks before the Presidential Election.

"As we begin this historic journey in the opening of the solar system to exploration, I want to personally thank President MacAdam for her staunch support of the Door Program. Her leadership has repeatedly opened the way of progress for our country and all the countries in the world.

Her decisive action to protect our country was demonstrated by her immediate and forceful retaliation to the attack of the initial launch of the Doorship One team.

She saved our lives. Thank you, Madam President.

I voted early and I voted for President Lacy MacAdam. It matters not which party, at this moment in history, what matters is for the country to have leadership that has been demonstrated, tried, and proven.

So, get out and vote and vote MacAdam," Joe said as Doorship One officially began its journey.

Wow, did you get any royalty for that departure speech," Darian commented afterwards.

"No, I just figured this was the moment for us to make an impact in the outcome of the election. For the next four years, I want to have the support we have so far enjoyed.

A new administration might want some immediate changes. I am hoping that we have made so much progress in the next few years that the Door program will be on automatic and supported by both parties," Joe replied.

"I just got a call from the President. She says thank you. You had an immediate impact on her ratings. They are going through the roof," Jorge communicated on the private channel.

Indeed, as Doorship One left orbit and headed toward the moon at roughly twenty-six thousand miles per hour the politics of the world were all being affected. The other launches and the work to assemble the remaining Doorships were now fully underway.

Doorship One neared the moon and would be moving into a new orientation.

"Are we ready with our back tracking laser setup? We will be getting into our exposed position in the next thirty minutes," Samantha said from her command chair.

Each of the team members had a similar seat in the command room. Every one of them had complete control from their position.

A green light indicated who had control. At the moment Joe still had the green light.

"OK, Yara, I believe you are the one coordinating this situation. I relinquish command," Joe said formally.

He got up and walked across the room to one of the ceiling ports that looked into the middle of the wheel.

The target area had been marked so it could be seen from the port window. He wondered if he would be able to see the laser beam when it hit the target area.

Deep in the jungle reservoir in Kenya the spotter called out, "the target is moving into position.

Shall we fire?"

"Let's make certain we are seeing the target side. Do we see the correct insignias?" another person at the laser cannon inquired of the technician on the twelve-inch telescope.

A third person on the laser cannon was at the cannon's aiming cross hairs that were part of an even bigger telescope. The system was computer controlled.

"Yes, we have the correct side being exposed," came back from the spotter.

The person at the controls activated the automatic firing sequence and watched. He was expecting to see a flash out in space.

"Here we go," he said into his mouthpiece.

"We have just been painted," Joe said as he saw the laser spot on the target area.

The beam was immediately back tracked with the Door One's laser. It was the spotting laser synchronized with seven strategically located missile launching ships and submarines.

"We have the location, are we a go," came the inquiry from the carrier JFK?

It was the oldest carrier still in service, but it was outfitted with the latest missile system. It additionally had a drone armada that could deliver more fire power than any ship in the world.

"It is a go," was the reply from the Chief of Staff as he got the nod from the President.

Two missiles lifted off.

A few moments later Joe declared, "I just saw a large cloud rise over the laser target area. I wonder who was behind this attack."

"That may be harder to find out than the elimination of the laser. I am also wondering why someone would want to suffocate us in our Doorship," R cubed voiced his thoughts.

"This effort seems to draw out adversaries for almost any and every reason. Some seem religious in nature, others just seem contrarian views and the willingness to take drastic action," Samantha said as she joined in the conversation.

The Presidential election was the day after the laser attack. The news about the laser attack and the President's direct intervention gave her a landslide victory. Her coat tails were long, and her party took control of the house and held the margin in the Senate at plus one. The President was in the best position political situation that she could have hoped for.

"I never dreamt that my pet project would be the fuel for my political efforts," she confided in her husband on the day of her victory.

This young man, Joe Elsinger seems to sense and take action to avert disaster. He and his wife Lydia provided me with the information to purge my leadership team. He has repeatedly handed me a situation that has improved my standing. His departure speech gave me almost a twenty-point gain in the poles.

I hope I get the chance to repay him," she continued.

"Well, you have taken some impressive action in support," her husband countered.

"Yes, I am glad that I decided to go with my gut feeling versus what my team said was the politically safe position. They were much more timid in what the responses should be," she replied.

The next order of business was to space test the Transmit-Receive units. The ones for the ship had been tested prior to departure. They would continue testing the units as the distances increased.

The unit designated for the moon was prepared as they approached the Moon. Its nuclear generator was powered up. They went through the transmit-receive startup sequence. Then they were ready for the trial test.

"OK, here comes the mouse," Tom declared as he punched the transmit switch.

"We have the mouse. We have the Mouse," Samantha declared as the mouse appeared in the receive chamber.

The mouse was quickly checked out and then put into the transmit chamber and sent back to Tom.

R cubed activated the transmission and a moment later they could hear Linda call our, "I have a mouse."

The transmit unit would be launched just prior to the arrival of the Doorship to its path around the Moon. A separate ground crew would take control and land it on the Moon at the designated landing site.

"We are approaching the Moon. Are we ready for the next attack," Joe inquired of the team?

He also keyed in a message to the Earth side part of the Door team.

"We are ready here," came back the reply.

The Door team was communicating on a private separate frequency. Whoever was involved in the sabotage of the environmental code was probably a member of the ground control team or had computer access to the system in some other way.

The signal to shut off the air supply came as the Doorship began its swing behind the moon. The response was to send back a packet of code to mark the source. It was designed to reproduce like a cancer to mark and to shut down the system it was in, but it would keep transmitting a location signal.

"Well, I am really curious where that packet will end up," Lydia voiced what the rest of the team was thinking.

Back on Earth, Aaron and Ryan were working with the tracking team to determine where the signal had come from. They were immediately able to determine that no one in the control room was involved. They followed the signal to a US location in Miami.

An FBI unit in Miami was called in and immediately proceeded to the building from which the homing signal was broadcasting.

They entered what was supposed to be a local reality business and caught the person still at the desk trying to clear her computer. It turned out she was the grandniece of Mathew Pinkerton III.

Even from his prison cell he had tried to get even with the President.

"I can't believe he was so vengeful that he was willing to kill six people," the President commented when she heard who had been involved.

"However, I wonder who else was involved," she continued.

She was going to follow her feelings on this matter. She believed it was deeper than just Mathew.

"Well, we have found the source of the signal. The person caught at the keyboard was none other than a grandniece of Mathew Pinkerton. The President has a full investigation underway to determine who else was involved," Jorge reported up to the Doorship One team.

"Well, I feel safe in the short term. However, we will take precautions here to ensure that no additional external influence can take control," Joe replied.

"What do you have in mind," Yara asked?

"I would like to have a totally isolated local control system. All external systems would be on an isolated system. The two would not be linked in any way. We could set up our communications system and monitoring system on the external system and all internal controls on the second one," Joe commented.

The other Doorships were assembled and put into full service with no additional issues. Their departures followed in order until all six were under way. One was headed inward toward the Sun. The other four would head outward toward their assigned planet. Meanwhile Doorship One had delivered the first Door to the moon. They would also deliver a Door to Mars as they used Mars to increase their speed toward the edge of the Solar system.

"I have been discussing the team rotation back to Earth with Tom, Linda and the General," Lydia brought up the subject at the team breakfast the next day.

"Tom and Linda would like to be the first to rotate up. This will be one of the few available moments of time they will have.

In a short time, the Door Ships will each be arriving at their designated planets and then the two of them will be fully consumed in checking out the doors as they are delivered.

Both Jorge and Jerry have voiced a desire to come up as well. They will most likely come up as a team. What order do we want to establish in our visits back to Earth," Lydia opened the discussion?

"I would like to schedule my trip back to coincide with my brother's wedding. It is six months from now," Yara spoke up.

"I will want to go with Yara," Darian added.

"Sam and I are flexible on the timing. We don't have anything special planned," R cubed joined in.

"Then Joe and I will take the first turn and be home for Christmas, our first anniversary and celebrate the New Year in Maui. I will work with all of you to plan a good rotation for all of us. We will want our plan to look out for the next several years," Lydia concluded the discussion.

Chapter 28 Payment in Full

Mathew Pinkerton III was well aware that prison time in the United States was intended to rehabilitate those individuals aberrant of the law. This presumed remorse on the part of the person found guilty. He had no remorse and he had made sure that his lawyers focused on getting him into a prison that would be a comfortable as possible.

His lawyers had done their job and he was in a minimum-security prison with great facilities. It had given him the time and the ability to plan and implement three ways to get back at the bitch of a President.

He was down to only four people directly helping him. His great nephew, his niece, and his old friend Victor.

Because of his superior intellect, he was sure he had enough fire power to defeat his arch enemy.

It took a full two weeks for him to learn about the failure of all of his schemes. He was shocked and stunned by his total failure.

He then learned of Madeline's and Victor's arrests.

"What magic does that Presidential witch woman have," he thought to himself as he made his daily walk?

His walk was interrupted by one of the guards.

"Mr. Pinkerton, I am to bring you in and get you ready for transfer," the guard said as he walked up.

"Transfer, what are you talking about," Mathew said in surprise?

"You are being indicted for crimes against the government," the guard informed him.

"I can't be retried for the same crime," Mathew replied as he was hand cuffed and led back toward the prison administrative office.

"You are correct, but they are trying you for premeditated intent to murder, conspiracy against the government and activities to incite riots," the guard informed Mathew.

"And by the way, I hope they convict you on every charge and put you so deep into the system that you rot in the dark. You have been such a spoiled, rotten prick while you've been here. The guards all cheered when we learned you were being charged," the guard volunteered.

At the same time as Mathew was being transferred, Madeline was being appraised of her situation by her lawyers. She sat in her orange prison outfit across the table from her lawyer.

"You are in serious trouble. You are facing life in prison if you are convicted in conspiring to down the launch vehicle with the Door crew on board. You are directly implicated in the attempt to disrupt the control of the environmental control system on board the Door Ship. Its looking really bad," her lawyer told her.

Madeline was having a hard time paying attention. How had they so easily captured her and then traced her actions and her connection to Victor? She knew Victor had also been arrested and was probably sitting in some similar office having a similar discussion with his lawyer.

"What are my options," Madeline inquired when she finally started to pay attention?

If you tell the entire story of your involvement in the attempts against the Door program, the prosecution is willing to settle for an attempted murder charge and twenty-five years in prison," her lawyer replied.

"Twenty-five years! I will be an old woman by the time I get out. Is that the best you can do," Madeline replied?

"Yes, that will be the best we can do. The actual time could be as short as six to eight years with parole if you are considered by the parole board as reformed and remorseful.

Madeline was already remorseful. She would not have to act that part. She really regretted getting caught. Hell would freeze over before she would be repentant or quit hating the bitch that was the President.

She took the deal.

When the successful deployment of the first Door and the continuing journey of Door Ship One toward Mars were reported on the news, Victor tried to make a call to Madeline, but her phone was answered by a stranger.

He quickly hung up, but Victor knew his days were numbered.

"It could even be only hours," he thought to himself.

"I can probably take my yacht and try to evade my ultimate arrest," he thought to himself.

He thought about it. Instead, he called a home moving agency and had them pack out his extensive wine collection and had it sent out to various family members and good friends.

Victor had never considered his nephew very talented, but he had always enjoyed discussing art with him. He had the Movers box up his small but valuable art collection and had it sent to the nephew.

He called his lawyer and told him he would soon need his services and arranged a meeting with him.

At the meeting he was informed that he could face a life sentence for his participation.

"Your job is to see if there is a way for me to cooperate and get a reduced sentence and assigned to a good prison," Victor had replied.

He was now seventy and he had resigned himself to dying in prison.

Victor carried his one remaining case of Cabernet Verite La Joie Sauvignon on board his yacht.

He made a couple of calls and invited two of his current young female friends to party on his yacht.

He threw on some steaks and fish on the grill and set the table for a late afternoon lunch.

He was relaxing under the white canvas covered deck with his two beauties when a dozen or so black official looking vehicles arrived at the main club house entrance building.

"Ladies, thanks for coming and keeping me company. It is time you left. Here, this is a key to a locker in the ladies room at the club house. There is a nice gift for each of you there," Victor said as he escorted them off the yacht.

He watched them sway their way up to the club house.

He returned to his lounge seat and took a sip of his wine and watched the armed contingent come down the pier toward his yacht. They were armed with their guns drawn and moving from cover to cover as if they were going to be met with a hail of bullets.

"They must think they are going to face an army," Victor thought to himself and took the last sip of his wine.

He got up and went to the gangway to greet the on-coming contingent.

Elena successfully made her escape from San Antonio.

She purchased a used vehicle for cash and drove to out of Texas toward the Northwest.

"I have always wanted to go trout fishing in the Teton area. This is a good time to do it," she thought to herself as she drove out of San Antonio on Interstate 10.

Her route took her north through to Abilene and then to Lubbock. There she stopped for a picnic lunch near the statue of Buddy Holly on the West Texas Hall of Fame walk. She was a fan of Holly's music and had made it a point to stop.

She took her time, driving carefully and in general relaxing. She knew better than to try and get out of the country through the normal routes. All her transactions were in cash, and she had processed her cash in San Antonio so that the bills were no longer straight out of her bank.

They were not going to trace her through her expenditures.

Those looking for her would not find her on any normal public transportation records or cameras.

She had dressed as a man to buy her used car.

She had changed the color of her hair and had dressed down.

That first day she stopped at a small hotel in Amarillo. She sold the car she had purchased in San Antonio. She went to a separate used car dealer and purchased another car.

The next day she made it to Salt Lake City and again stayed at a non-descript Mom and Pop hotel. She again sold her car for cash and went to a separate used car lot and bought another.

She knew that the temporary plates would take a long time to show up in any of the state records. Eventually those looking might be able to trace her via her used cars, but she hoped to be long gone when they finally figured out her route.

She spent one afternoon trout fishing in Idaho and then she made her final run in the US up highway 93 and stopped at Roseville, Idaho. Here she donated her car to a Goodwill shop.

She dressed in a hiking outfit she had purchased in San Antonio. After a couple of days, she left in the evening and hiked across the border into Canada. She signed in legally at a hiker's border crossing booth.

Elena felt really lucky when she was picked up by a trucker going to Vancouver.

"I am willing to pay for the ride," she had volunteered. She did not want any other situation to crop up.

"Lady, you are a fresh breeze for me. I do this trip about two times a month and it is a killer. Your company will make all the difference," he had responded.

By the time they arrived in Vancouver Elena had heard about every problem Lane, the truck driver was experiencing. This included an on again, off again love affair he was having with a young lady named Diane in Vancouver.

"Look, here is a gift for you so you can take Diane out to a good restaurant. Tell her that you really do care for her. Just be yourself," Elena coached him.

"Thanks. And thanks for listening to me for the last two days," Lane responded.

Leaving Vancouver was a touchy point. She bought her ticket to Christ Church, New Zealand under a different name and passport. She hoped that this identity had not been compromised.

She was now Selena Mondeles an artist from Mataro, Spain. She was able to book a flight out on the following day. She would have loved to make the trip in first class but did not want to be that noticed. She also made sure to wire her money to the Bank of New Zealand in Christ Church. She did not want to get caught by a lie on the question, "Are you carrying more than $10,000 into the country?"

The flight down was long and boring. She slept almost all the way. She cleared the New Zealand customs and then took a local flight from Wellington to Christchurch. She had taken a rental with the Blackwood Bed and Breakfast Place on Strout Street. This was close to the Waimai Beach Golf Course and the Pacific Ocean.

Within the week she had established an account at the Bank of New Zealand and had made the connection to the bank holding the ten million she had earned for her Door assignment. This she had transferred to another offshore account. She closed the account she had just transferred the money from.

"If possible, I am going to focus on becoming a teacher, playing golf and enjoying surfing," Elena now Selena thought to herself as she walked the beach as the early morning sun came up over the sea.

Elena would never be found. She became a great teacher. She never married.

Chapter 29: Tom and Linda's Surprise

The afterglow of success is often accompanied with a letdown. Success has a surge that pushes feelings to unexpected highs. The outward flow of this surge pulls the reservoir of emotions down. Sometimes the pull is down to unexpected lows.

Tom never suffered this cycle. Since the day he had almost fallen off the bar stool when Linda had made her lifelong pass at him, he had enjoyed being frozen emotionally at a high.

Seeing Joe's head look up at the helicopter after the kidnapping was a high.

Having his daughters make him and Linda grandparents was a high.

Hearing Joe's voice once he had made it into the control module in space was a high.

Watching the successful landing of the first Door on the moon was a high.

All the events in the last several years kept bumping Tom's emotional reservoir higher. The only threat was if the reservoir dam were to break.

The test of the Moon Door immediately sparked an idea in Tom's head that he could not let go. He and Linda had designed in an automatic transmit control system for all the Doors.

He was taking a hot, lazy morning, shower, singing one of his bawdy beer drinking songs when the thought came to him, "I can be the mouse and travel to the Moon any time I want, or to Mars."

Tom rushed into the kitchen singing, "Fly me to the moon," written by Bart Howard and made famous by Frank Sinatra.

Tom finished singing his modified version and then gave Linda a full kiss across her lips.

"I knew the stress of the last few months would take its toll," Linda said as Tom followed up with a hug.

"Oh, I have gone crazy, that is for sure. You and I are going to the Moon. Then we are going to Mars. Then we are going out to Doorship One," Tom said as he guided Linda around in a jig.

"What has come over you," Linda said as she gave her typical Tom what in the world has come over you laugh.

"Well, I was thinking about my little test mouse. If it was smart enough it could come and go as it pleased. We are smarter than a mouse and we can go to the Moon and anywhere else as we please and stay as little or as long as we please," Tom replied.

"We have been talking to Lydia about going out to Doorship One. Why not see the Moon and Mars on the way," Tom said?

He accepted his two over easy eggs, three strips of bacon and a biscuit and took a large bite. He raised his eyebrows in his "don't you think that's a great idea" look.

"Will we be able to convince Jorge and the rest of the team," Linda said as she sat down across from Tom with her breakfast and cup of tea?

"Oh, leave that to me," Tom said with a wink and a smile.

"You want to do what," Jorge said about an hour later as the team sat around reviewing the Door program progress?

"I want to take the long way out to Door Ship One. We need to test and set up the Moon base. Linda and I can be the first to go. We can receive the first few Moon settlers. Then we can transmit to Mars and do the same startup there. This will test four paths, Earth to Moon, Moon to Mars, Earth to Mars and finally Mars to Door Ship One," Tom replied in an energetic way.

"What about, the Earth to Door Ship One, and Moon to Doorship One," Jacqueline inquired?

"The beauty of this is that each of us going out to Doorship One can choose a route and all routes can be tested," Linda joined in as she got excited by Tom's enthusiasm.

"I think this idea has some merit," Aaron said in his polite quiet way.

"I like the idea. But first, can I get a trial transmission here on the base," Jerry chimed in?

He was still a little nervous about the technology and wanted to have his feet on the Earth for his first experience.

"Yes, Yes, we can do that today," Tom said as he reached up and gave Jerry a shoulder hug.

"Ryan, you have been working with Lydia on a Doorship One rotation schedule for us. Incorporate Tom's ideas and get the locations each of us plan to travel through.

"You win and by the way Tom, I am quite willing to let you be the first mouse through to each of these locations. I am still worried about the light diffraction over the distances across the solar system," Jorge commented with a smile.

"Ah, yes, did Linda tell you about her beam refocusing algorithm. She tells me she can make me quite handsome if I am kind to her," Tom replied with a smile and a wink.

A few weeks later Tom could be heard from the Moon, "I am the mouse; yes indeed, I am the mouse."

Two weeks later the same call came through from Mars.

Then the call came in from Doorship One, we have the mouse, we have the mouse or is it a Rat? Lydia said as Tom arrived. Linda followed a few moments later.

A day later, Joe and Lydia were on their way back to Earth.

"Well team, see you in a month or so," Lydia commented as she got into the transmit chamber.

Both Joe and Lydia were invited to the White House for a visit.

"Why don't you join us in our remote ranch location for a brief respite? Uncle Ted claims he will give you a meal fit for a Queen," Joe replied to the invitation.

The last thing he wanted to do was go to DC and to get discovered by the media.

The journey outward would take years to accomplish. The Door technology provided a way for humans to advance into the Universe at a speed humans were capable of accomplishing.

There would be continued learn, improvements and change and everyone involved would grow and mature. They would all have a rich life.

THE END

About the Author
Ronald E. Mueller
remwriter95@gmail.com

Ron has a fascination with the scientific thought process. He writes stories just beyond the possible but clearly achievable with just the right technological breakthrough.

Ron's science fiction almost seems true. His heroes are not superhuman but rather the regular guy put into a must do situation. These must do characters are of all genders and races. The bad guys are equally diverse.

Ron's background as a control system engineer and production system optimization has exposed him to how equipment is made. He is a professional engineer and has been around most of the developing technology of the day.

Ron was born in Brazil, grew up in Iowa, served in Vietnam, graduated from the University of South Florida, worked for Procter and Gamble for thirty-seven years and has been happily married for forty-three years.

He is the father of three great offspring and now the grandfather of three grandchildren.

First Name	Family Name	Role
Aaron	Alton	Genius Programmer
Alice		Alice's House Cleaning and Maid Service
Brenda		kidnaper
Craig	Lebak	Secretary of State
Darian		one of human Guinee pigs
Devnid	Krupin	Russian Fold team member
Doug	Hasterly	Security officer
Elena		Independent for hire spy
Fang	Zhin Xiao	Chinese astronaut
Fred		RV owner
Jorge	Martinez	General Leading the effort
Gupta	Kumar	India's Fold team member
Harold	Muller	German Fold team member
Harold	Hatfield Hastly	H cubed new recruit to the program
He-Ping	Ye	Chinese astronaut
Jacqueline	Hazley	psychologist
Jason		kidnaper
Jeffrey	Chang	China Fold team member
Jerry	Delaney	US Marine Core General transport ships
Joe	Pender Elsinger	main character
John		Truck driver
Lacy	MacAdam	President
Leatrice		Waitress at the truck stop
Lester		kidnaper
Lydia	Jade Tabata	Joe's companion
Madeline		Mathew's great niece
Manfredo	Silva	Brazil's Fold team member
Mathew	Pinkerton III	Secretary of Defense her arch enemy
Matt		kidnaper
Max		kidnaper
Muhyi	al Din Hakimi	Blade of Justice
Nancy		RV owner
Ryan	McComber	Project manager
Sheng	Zang	Chinese astronaut
Stanley	Black	science advisor to the President
Sylvester	Sloan	Known as Phil
Tom-Linda		Great Britain Fold team members
Trey	Elsinger	Joe's father
Uncle Ted		Like a second father to Joe
Victor	Montique	Friend of Mathew's that helped him
Yara		new recruit to the program

Published by: Around the World Publishing LLC.

www.ingramcontent.com/pod-product-compliance
Lightning Source LLC
Chambersburg PA
CBHW060226100726
47907CB00003B/521